It's the wedding day but where's the bride?

"Paul." Peter Hamilton's troubled voice broke into his son's sea of turmoil. "It's time to file a missing persons report."

Paul shoved his chair back from the desk that overflowed with paperwork needing his attention. "I know. I've held off until today hoping she'd come back or call. Our wedding day. What a farce. I'm here worried sick and only God knows where she is, fighting battles we can only imagine!"

"Steady, boy." Love shone in the dark eyes that looked so like his son's. "God *does* know where she is and we can take comfort from that."

CONNIE LORAINE, pen name of a well-established novelist, always wanted to write and always wanted to be a nurse. Despite her choice of career, her life-long interest in nursing is put to good use when she writes, as she does frequently, about nurses, doctors, and hospitals.

Lamp
in Darkness

Connie Loraine

Shepherd of Love Hospital Series: Book One

Heartsong Presents

ISBN 1-55748-558-5
LAMP IN DARKNESS

PRINTED IN THE U.S.A.

prologue

Seattle fog curled into the city's streets like a kitten twined around a beloved owner's legs. Wisps and drifts softened street lights and muted brilliant neat piles of autumn leaves waiting to be gathered and recycled. The mournful howl of a Puget Sound ferry coming in from Bainbridge Island added an eerie touch and reminded Seattle's inhabitants Halloween lurked just a few days away.

Nicholas Fairchild stood at the window of his clifftop mansion and surveyed the scene. Some of the night's loneliness crept into his soul. Sixty-five, still vigorous and one of the wealthiest men in Washington state, his mood matched the fog, despite a softly lit, luxurious room and the cheerful flames of a gas log fireplace. His lips twisted. Pollution alerts had banned the use of wood fires. How he missed seeing great logs burning in the huge fireplace, their sweet-smelling smoke scenting his home. Progress to many people and the need for clean air meant sacrificing some things for the good of many.

Nicholas turned from the window and sharply closed the custom draperies but he could not shut out the feeling of desolation he carried or his own personal ghosts. Always one to go to the crux of a problem he sat down in a leather chair, stared into the small fire and into himself. "God, I've spent all my life amassing a fortune.

I'm respected for working hard, being honest and refusing to take advantage of others. Am I feeling this way just because of the fog? Or are You trying to tell me something?" He shifted weight, reached for a switch and noiselessly shut off all the lights. A rosy glow from the fire painted his grey hair auburn and showed the planes and hollows of his not handsome, yet interesting face, with its changing expressions.

Perhaps if he had married—Nicholas shook his head. The only woman he had ever cared for had died before they could share their dreams. His sensitive mouth compressed into a grim line. Did all men who reached the top find it this lonely? How many years lay ahead and what would he do with them?

Nicholas turned to his unfailing source of strength. "If there is something You want me to do, Lord, more than what I already am, please guide me. In Jesus' name, amen."

After a long moment he stood and slowly trod thick carpeting to his bedroom. His gaze turned to the bookcase that covered an entire wall and provided an alternative to sleepless nights. He hesitated, then selected Catherine Marshall's tribute to her husband, who had been chaplain of the United States Senate in the late 40's, as well as a preacher like few others. *The Best of Peter Marshall*'s pages fell open to a story Nicholas had read and pondered many times: "By Invitation of Jesus."

Nicholas showered, made ready for bed and began to read, feeling he had unexpectedly paid a visit to old friends.

How like he was to that fictional man in the other

Washington, sitting in his comfortable home with a rising wind! How similar their social positions, their desire to live godly lives, their realization life should be more than money, power or prestige. Nicholas caught his breath as if he had never heard the story. He followed the account of the other man feeling a presence come into the room; how he realized how far short his banquets and dinners fell from the one described in Luke 14, the one where Jesus told his hearers to call to a feast the poor, maimed, lame and blind, not those who could repay the giver. His heart again thrilled to the invitation of the man in the story, the bidding that began, *JESUS OF NAZARETH requests the honor of your presence...*

Nicholas closed the book, needing no more reading to refresh his memory of a story he knew by heart. The Washington man had literally followed Jesus' command. He had filled his mansion with those of the streets, those who needed him—and Christ—most.

A familiar stirring quickened the troubled man's weary mind and swept boredom and sadness from his heart. He rose and crossed to the window, expecting to find the fog had lifted. It had not. Thick and grey, it blanketed the city except for the spire of a large cathedral not far from the Fairchild mansion. Skillfully lighted, it pointed the way to heaven for those who took the time to look up and beyond earth and its woes.

Nicholas watched the spire until fatigue sent him to bed and sleep. Did the fog, the story, the spire combine with his prayer for guidance, his longing to make the latter years even more of a witness to his risen Lord than his earlier days? He never knew. He only knew that in his dreams he wandered fogged-in Seattle streets until he reached the stone steps of the nearby cathedral. Figures, huddled and erect, proud and beaten, grouped on the steps and clutched at his clothing as he struggled up through the crowd trying to ascend the eternal stair- case. His dream shifted. The steeple vanished, but the stairway went on. He recognized many who also toiled upwards. Sometimes they slipped and fell. "Oh, help them!" he wanted to cry, but no words came. He stooped, took a downtrodden soul by the arm and encouraged him to climb. The friendly support made all the difference. Around him, others followed Nicho- las' example. Person began to help person until many were lifted from their places and brought higher.

The fog faded. Nicholas opened his blue eyes to a new day and skies that smiled. Where were the ennui and dread that had accompanied his recent wakings? Where was the desire to turn over, drown himself in sleep and escape facing another monotonous repeat of the days before?

"Thank You, God." He stretched and threw wide the curtains of his soul. "I still don't know exactly what You want of me but whatever it is, I'm ready."

During the early winter months, Nicholas Fairchild sought his Lord in mighty prayer. He studied the Bible, especially the passages where Jesus gave admonition and instruction. He also realized one day most of his studies had narrowed to the book of Luke, the Great Physician. An idea whose magnitude and daring would call forth every ounce of energy, all the resources Nicho- las could muster, seeded itself in his brain and heart. He spoke of it to no one except God, as was his custom when contemplating a new venture.

A week before Christmas he felt the time had come. Like Peter Marshall's rich man, Nicholas chuckled at the expression on his associates' faces when they read what he asked to be sent to a hundred leading men and women in the city of Seattle. First came shock. Next, disbelief. Then, a quick look at their employer. Finally, the unswerving loyalty of employees to employer who long had made them feel they worked *with* Fairchild, not just for him.

Two days later, his missives hit like hailstones. One hundred recipients of hand-delivered messages gaped when they read the words, patterned after those in "By Invitation of Jesus."

> *JESUS CHRIST invites you to a meeting of great importance on Christmas Eve, 8:00 p.m. at the residence of Nicholas Fairchild. RSVP*

"Christmas Eve!" Physicians and architects, attorneys and contractors, bankers and ministers groaned in protest. Had Fairchild gone mad, calling a meeting at such a time? Rumor buzzed like saws in a lumber mill yet affirmative responses poured in. With the exception of a few renowned medical personnel with critical cases, all summoned came.

Nicholas welcomed them on a rainy Chritmas Eve that contrasted sharply with the light and warmth inside his home. His servants had arranged space by throwing wide the enormous doors between library, living and drawing rooms. Comfortable chairs welcomed the curious, half-resentful guests. One, more familiar with the host than most, voiced their unanimous unspoken question, "Why have you summoned us and in such a strange manner?"

"Fellow citizens, I have decided to build a hospital and I need your help."

Mouths dropped open and a dozen voices cried, "A hospital? Seattle has a multitude of hospitals, many known worldwide. Fred Hutchinson Cancer Research Center, Children's, Harborview, Providence, Swedish, the University of Washington's Medical Center, and a dozen more."

Nicholas straightened his spare frame. "I know. But I have to build a hospital." He saw scorn and skepticism in their faces. "All those you mentioned and others are matchless and I hope my new venture will be affiliated with them and use their services often. But this one will be like no other—anywhere."

"Why?" someone asked after a few seconds of stunned silence.

He braced against their inevitable reaction. "First, no patient will ever be refused care, no matter how long term or extensive, on the basis of ability to pay."

He ignored the shocked ripple of sound and plunged on.

"Second, the finest medical personnel only will be considered and salaries will be above the norm." He drew a deep breath. "There will, however, be one qualification every person from head surgeon to janitor must meet and that is to be an active, practicing Christian who combines humankind's best skills with intense prayer."

"You can't make that stick," a deep voice criticized. "The government won't stand for that kind of discrimination."

Nicholas smiled a curious smile. He had anticipated every objection. "This hospital will in no way be connected with the government. Neither will it receive grants. To do so would open it up to legal restrictions and defeat its purpose."

"It will take millions!"

"I have them." Nicholas quietly surveyed the watching faces.

Some looked mildly interested. Others raised their eyebrows and exchanged glances. A few faces showed recognition of what such a place could mean to those persons Nicholas spoke of.

"Think of it. A hospital whose portals are carved with scriptural promises. A place that is less an institution and more a haven. A staff who begins each shift fresh from a prayer service where each patient is brought before the throne of God. A group of individuals bound together and to their work by One Chief." The memory of his dream and subsequent searching filled his voice with pleading and he spread wide his hands. "I believe it can be done. No, I believe it will be done. You can help if you choose, but with or without you, this hospital is going to be built."

For a minute his sincerity echoed from the walls and hushed even the most disbelieving but not for long.

"Fairchild, you can't even get land in Seattle for a hospital," a certain developer declared as he waved his arms.

"That's right," a city planner added. "Even if you

could, you'll be stopped dead in the water by zoning laws, not to mention environmental impact statements and a dozen other things."

Again came the curious smile and glint in their host's eyes that boded inside knowledge. Nicholas walked to a nearby table, picked up a worn Bible that lay open and prepared.

"Matthew 6:33-34.* 'But seek ye first the kingdom of God, and his righteousness; and all these things shall be added unto you. Take therefore no thought for the morrow: for the morrow shall take thought for the thing of itself. Sufficient unto the day is the evil thereof.' Could anything be nearer the kingdom of God and His righteousness than a temple of prayer and medicine whose doors beckon all who need to come unto them—and to Him?"

"You actually expect *God* to provide the land, waive all the regulations and pave the way for you to build this charity hospital?" the developer demanded. "Fairchild, I didn't think any grown man in the 1990s could be that naive."

Strangely, no one laughed—except Nicholas, who held up the Bible.

"We're also told to become little children, trusting and expectant," he said to his fascinated audience who had forgotten it was Christmas Eve in the bizarre twist the meeting had taken. "I tell you, if this plan is of God—and I will stake my reputation and everything I own that it is—no power can prevent its completion."

"I'll lay ten to one odds that your Nicholas Fairchild Hospital will never be built," challenged a TV reporter, who had suspected something unusual would take place

*KJV

at Fairchild's and slipped in uninvited with the guests.

"I'll lay you a million to one odds it won't," Nicholas fired back, to the consternation of the crowd who, in spite of themselves, showed a growing belief the thing was possible, although not probable.

"What is this, a hoax?" The reporter didn't give an inch. Disgust dripped from her sharp tongue. "Nice thing, bring all these people here on Christ's birthday just to preach at them then back down."

The commanding presence that had taken Nicholas from humble beginnings to his current position made him loom taller and more formidable than ever.

"Madam, you said the Nicholas Fairchild Hospital will never be built. I only agreed. Do you think I would demean myself and to name a place such as I have described after me or any other man or woman?" His blue eyes darkened with righteous indignation. "Must I remind you that while I will serve to the best of my ability in an advisory capacity, I will never be the Chief?"

The woman clutched her purse with tense fingers but her training and experience in ferreting out stories served her well.

"Then what is this—fantasy—to be called?"

A smile that erased everything but a humbleness not always found in influential leaders made Nicholas' craggy face almost handsome.

"It will be known as the Shepherd of Love Hospital and engraved beside each door will be words taken from the 23rd Psalm,* 'The Lord is my shepherd. . .though I walk through the valley of the shadow of death, I will fear no evil.'"

Even the wave of approval that swept the assembly

*KJV

could not still the avid reporter who anticipated a pay raise for this story.

"Isn't that misleading? You aren't going to guarantee that every patient will be cured, are you?" She paused, then added, "Why, if you do, the other hospitals might as well close down immediately."

"The Shepherd of Love Hospital will not claim the power of life or death. It ultimately rests with the Chief." Nicholas' lips trembled at the significance of the simple statement. "Yet I do expect a high success rate. Any of the leading physicians who are here tonight can tell you a patient's mental attitude plays a far greater part in the healing process than most people realize. By talking with patients, reassuring them and praying with them as they permit, our staff will be going far beyond the usual means to help prepare patients for what lies ahead."

Several leading doctors nodded.

"You said *they permit*," the reporter stuck as close to every word as a bloodhound to a trail. "This implies you expect to serve other than just Christian patients."

Nicholas astounded her and the others with a ringing laugh. "Sinners, saints and all in-between will be welcomed," he solemnly replied, although his eyes twinkled in their bright blueness. "Didn't our Master invite all to come to Him? The only requirement will be that those who do come need help—physical, emotional, mental or spiritual."

When eyebrows raised, he added, "Oh, yes, we will have chaplains and counselors for those who are hurting other than in their bodies."

He waited for more questions. When none came, he

quietly told his guests, "I know you feel I may be stray-
ing from my senses. I'm not. I intend to go into this
project the same way I have done with other projects
all my life. Perhaps I have only really come to my senses
and to a realization of the need Seattle has for the Shepherd of Love Hospital."

They left in little groups, to homes and belated Christmas Eve celebrations to spread the word and muse over
what they had heard. In closing Nicholas had assured
them they would never be asked for money, only for
goodwill and prayers. If some chose to contribute time
or finances, it must be as a result of their own beliefs in
the project and its underlying principles. Caught between this man's record of success in all he did and
their own doubts it could ever happen, those who had
attended the meeting passed on their differing views to
others.

Seattle rocked when the TV reporter's version burst
into the homes of the city's residents. She scrupulously
stuck to the facts but couldn't help ending with an edi-
torial comment, "Such a vision as the one presented
may appear believable in this season of goodwill and
peace on earth. In reality, it will in all probability become known as Nicholas Fairchild's one great folly.
Goodnight and happy holidays."

"Fairchild's Folly" stuck as a nickname. Yet when
weeks ran into months, Seattle marveled. A recluse
who owned a huge chunk of property on a wooded hill
overlooking the Sound emerged from the carved wood-
work of his library. To the dismay of his expectant heirs,
he deeded the entire property to Nicholas with the stipulation it be used for the unusual hospital he had read

about. He further astounded the city by turning over most of his vast fortune to the future hospital, reserving only enough to keep him comfortably in a private retirement home until the Shepherd of Love was completed, at which time he would take up permanent residence in a quiet wing he insisted be added for "old codgers" like him.

Amazement turned to wonder when Nicholas and the small but dedicated corps of those who prayed and accepted the work as God's will breezed through the formalities of legal work.

One year from the first meeting, a grateful Nicholas turned over the first shovelful of earth, with reporters stumbling over themselves for pictures. Word had spread throughout the country about the aim, purpose and determination of "Fairchild's Folly." When unasked-for checks poured in, foundations became fact and a bevy of electricians, plumbers, and builders haunted the site from dawn to dusk, Seattle awakened from its derision and believed.

By the second Christmas Eve, the hospital's long, low buildings spread across the donated land. Winter sunlight turned the white stone walls to cream and glinted off windows that sparkled with loving care. Sixty-seven, and younger in mind and spirit than he had been for years, Nicholas took a final, solitary trek from one building to another, all joined by covered passages. Shining steel instruments were sterilized and waiting for surgeons' hands that would be used with full realization of the One who guided them. Pastel-painted rooms with empty beds and attractive curtains stood in cleanliness. At Nicholas' insistence, no part of the hospital stood more than two stories high. Now he admired the gleaming corridors as he walked them. A lump rose in his throat. Tomorrow in a public, well attended ceremony the Shepherd of Love Hospital would be dedicated and the Chief recognized. Tonight Nicholas felt the Presence of that Chief. Not a single decision had been made without seeking God in prayer. Surely a hospital so conceived, so carried out, would fulfill its dual purpose: to heal the sick and to bring souls to a knowledge of the living Christ.

. . .*and God saw that it was good.**

Nicholas knelt in the empty hallway, filled with gratitude and deep humility. "Oh, Lord, I know how You felt when You created heaven and earth. Please, help me and those who come here, whether to heal or to be healed, to always remember this work is not of our making but a gift from You. We are your tools, God. Keep us polished, bright and worthy. I ask these things in Jesus' name, amen."

On Christmas Day, the Shepherd of Love Hospital opened its doors to a crowd of curious Seattleites who swarmed through the new building, peered into its every corner, and ran exploring fingers over the Bible verses carved here and there, impressive in their simplicity.

Three years later, Jonica Carr came to the hospital.

---

*Genesis 1:10 (KJV)

one

*Thy word is a lamp unto my feet, and a light unto my path.**

"What a strange inscription to grace the door of a hospital director's office!" Jonica Carr thought. She paused, took a deep breath and chastised herself. Now that the moment she had waited ten years for had arrived, why should she tremble? What did it matter that although she vaguely recognized the quotation, she couldn't reconcile it with the medical field?

She rubbed damp hands together and dried them with a tissue from her carelessly worn shoulder bag. The action brought a vision of herself at fifteen, nervously perspiring and waiting for the first and only boy who had ever asked her out.

Anguish rolled over her as if it were yesterday. The shy boy's arrival. Her father's rage. Subsequent days, weeks, and years of high school walled off from classmates by pride that permitted no pity, only hatred for her strong, five-foot-ten-inch, one hundred and fifty pound body.

Did the timid teenager she thought she'd left behind still live inside? Jonica brushed aside the thought and squared her shoulders under the soft blue blazer that matched both her eyes and the pleated skirt of her suit. She no longer walked stooped over, ashamed of her body. Superb health and determination born of

*Psalm 119:105 (KJV)

desperation had brought her far from that long-ago night when she vowed to become someone, to escape her abusive home and make it on her own. She remembered the envious looks of classmates when her top grades won her a full scholarship in nursing, her chosen field. Jonica had breezed through the four-year university course with honors, while some of her fellow graduates settled for the two-year LPN course, then work and just the dream of returning for BS degrees and RN status.

Still hesitating outside the director's office, Jonica rapidly reviewed her upward climb. She'd been unwilling to become lost in the shuffle of an enormous hospital so accepted a position in a small Tacoma hospital that recognized hard work and skill. Her big break came—literally—during Jonica's third year when the night shift charge nurse was suddenly called away because her father was injured in a fall.

"Put Carr in charge," she told the powers-that-be. "I'll only be gone a week and it isn't worth getting someone in who isn't used to how we do things. Besides, except for emergencies, how many surgeries are scheduled between eleven and seven?" In that week, followed by another when the charge nurse's father became worse, Jonica ran things so smoothly the surgical department manager saw her potential and promptly ordered that she be considered for training for a charge nurse's duties. Months later, the charge nurse position became vacant. The ambitious second-in-command relished the dilemma the hospital faced, with the entire surgical department clamoring for her to get the job while administration openly doubted that any twenty-four-year-old could handle such a responsible position. They compromised by assigning her the duties and the title for a probationary period of six months—and fell over themselves at the end of her trial months with praise and admiration for her calm, unruffled demeanor that reassured patients and staff alike. Jonica overheard the Chief of Staff comment he'd never seen "such a cool cucumber as Carr in emergencies."

"May I help you?"

A deep masculine voice jerked her back to the present. She whipped around. A tallish, slim man with white streaks in his hair and eyes as blue as her own stood smiling at her.

"I—was just going in." She put her hand to the doorknob and couldn't help adding, "I'm Jonica Carr, the new night charge nurse in surgery."

An odd expression crossed the older man's face. "It's a pleasure to meet you. Welcome to Shepherd of Love."

"Thank you." She noticed how young and alive he looked when his smile broadened. "Do you work here?"

He nodded and gallantly swung the door inward for her. "I'll be seeing you again, Miss Carr. Or is it Mrs.? Or Ms.?"

She glanced both ways and whispered, "Miss, but I like Jonica best." He bowed and swung off down the highly polished corridor, stopping now and then to admire the continuing mural of sea, forest and mountains that brightened the walls.

"He loves this place," she murmured. It seemed a good omen, as had the friendliness of the staff when she had applied for her new job just a few weeks earlier, not expecting to get it but confident she could do it well if chosen. She knocked on the closed door.

"Come in, Miss Carr." The hospital director rose from behind his practical desk, a style in keeping with the paneled walls and muted carpeting. A view of an early-summer Puget Sound through an open window brought a fresh breeze and cooled Jonica's flushed face. "We feel fortunate to have you join us." When she couldn't hide her surprise, he smiled. She liked his keen eyes, modest dress and obvious efficiency tempered by caring. "Oh, yes, I make it a point to know each of the staff personally. If there is ever anything you need, do not hesitate to come tome. You'll notice I prefer to be personally available rather than use a secretary as a buffer. Now," he changed to brisk business. "We chose you despite your youth and limited charge nurse experience because of several factors. First, your record is impeccable. Even more important, yourdeportment at your personal interview showed clearly your ability to maintain your composure under trying circumstances." He smiled again. "Interviewing for a position, even at Shepherd of Love, or perhaps I should say especially at Shepherd of Love, can be trying." He shuffled papers and paused. "Only one question on your application had a rather sketchy answer but I'm sure that's due to our shortsightedness in not leaving enough room to write everything you'd like."

Her heart plummeted. She knew what question this observing man meant. It had taken her longer to respond to the simple query, *Are you a Christian?* than to fill in the rest of the lengthy form. Hadn't her penned words, *Yes. I was baptized as a teenager and have been faithful in attending church except when on duty,* been enough? If not, why had they waited until now to question her on it? Surely she wouldn't be disqualified now that official notice of her appointment had come and she'd served her thirty-day notice in Tacoma!

"You are a Christian, aren't you?" the kindly director prodded.

"Of course." She certainly wasn't a heathen. She believed in God and accepted Jesus as His Son. If sometimes she felt God was some faraway Power Who had little interest in her, she need not confess it.

Her quick reply appeared to settle any doubts the director might harbor. He rose, shook hands, then asked, "Did you tour the hospital when you were here before?"

"Oh, yes!" She knew eagerness sent a glow to her face. "It's perfect—large enough to have the best equipment yet small enough to feel almost like a family home." Wistfulness crept into her voice.

"Do you think you can be happy with us?"

She sobered. "I know I can." She blinked and scoffed at the instant moisture crowding her eyes. She never cried, hadn't since she ran away from home all those years ago, from the stepfather she hated, the pretty but weak mother whose only defense against him was a threat to leave if he ever touched Jonica in any way. In rapid-fire order a series of temporary dwelling places flashed through her mind: shelters, when available; doorways when shelters weren't; studying at libraries and working in fast-food restaurants; her first rented room—in a miserable dump just one step above the street. How she had begrudged the time work took from school and studying! A less determined person would have given up and dropped out. She did neither. She also learned to thank whatever God there might be for her height and weight. Twice they had helped her out of danger when men approached her.

"I-I never really had a home until I went to college," she said.

"You have one now, Miss Carr." He walked into the hall with her and again she wanted to cry. "Are you settled into your quarters?"

She nodded, not trusting herself to speak.

He patted her shoulder as he would have done had she been a favorite daughter. She did not shrink from his touch, as she'd learned to do when some colleagues acted too friendly. Unless she were totally mistaken about people—and her years of fighting for survival in a hostile world had developed inner awareness beyond the ordinary—only goodness filled her new boss.

Did he divine her thoughts? "Remember, Miss Carr, I'm only the hospital director. God is our Chief." He smiled again and vanished inside his office, leaving the door standing open. She had the feeling it normally stayed open; perhaps it had blown shut today before she came.

Fifteen minutes later she luxuriated in a warm shower. She had settled into the charming combination bed-sitting room with kitchenette and bath attached to the hospital and offered at nominal cost to those employees who wished to live on the grounds. The small suites were located in a separate building at the farthest point from the ambulance entry where a stand of giant trees and colorful flowerbeds muted the noise. In addition, acoustical tile ensured additional quiet.

Jonica's particular suite sported off-white walls, a deep

blue rug and matching draperies. She had chosen it over
a counterpart done in yellows and gratefully rejoiced
the rooms were tastefully furnished. Her struggle to
succeed had left little time to accumulate furniture, even
if she'd had a place to keep it. An end unit, her suite
faced north, with a view of more trees and gardens from
the bed-sitting room at one end. A large window at the
west showed white-capped Puget Sound. The kitchenette and bath each had a small window, screened for
safety, that overlooked more of the well-tended grounds.

"And he wondered if I could be happy here!" Jonica
repeated while she toweled her thick, medium brown
hair, then coaxed it into the simple, pulled-back style
that suited her so well, with a slight turn under at the
nape of her neck. She added a touch of lipstick, the
only makeup she ever wore, and deliberately surveyed
her image—not pretty or glamorous, but clean and fresh-
looking with lovely, clear skin untouched by beauty aids.
Donning an aqua skirt and blouse outfit, she suddenly
grinned. "Not bad at all." She blew a kiss at her reflection, slipped into white sandals, reached for a matching
purse, and headed toward the small private dining room
where she had eaten the day she was interviewed. En-
joying the day, she soaked in the sunshine and the laughter that came from a group of off-duty nurses grouped
in comfortable chairs outside the staff quarters.

"Come join us," one called. "You're Jonica Carr, aren't
you? If you're half the wonder woman rumor has it,
Shepherd of Love's really blessed to get you!"

Jonica searched the greeting for a sting and found
none. She found herself eager to get off to the right
start with these women, some of whom could be in her

charge.

"I can see my press agent's been here doing a good job," she said lightly and felt delighted at the laughs it brought.

The friendly nurses evidently found her acceptable. A strange pang went through the newcomer. All through college and training, even at Tacoma, she'd been too busy getting ahead to make many close friends. One of the nicest things about working at Shepherd of Love might be having that opportunity. She sat down beside a dark-skinned nurse whose twinkly dark eyes laughed even when her lips remained straight. She looked about Jonica's age.

"Nancy Galbraith. We're glad to have you here." Warmth radiated from her simple greeting. "Pediatrics."

"Patty Thompson, Outpatient," said the blond who had first spoken.

"Shina Ito, Obstetrics." The tiny Japanese girl pronounced it *sheena*.

"What an unusual name. I like it," Jonica said impulsively.

"It means good, virtuous," Patty put in. "She's too modest to say so."

"You could take a lesson from her," the final member of the group heckled.

"I am modest. Shina's just modester—oh dear, there's no such word, is there?" Patty pretended embarrassment but Jonica saw how her eyes twinkled. "At least I introduced myself."

"I'm Lindsey Best," the freckled, redhead said with a wide grin. "I don't have to say anything more with that name, right?"

Jonica felt as if she'd had a second warm shower. "Right. Where do you work?"

The irrepressible Lindsey who rivaled Patty in clowning (but turned out to be an excellent nurse) put on a fake drawl and opened her green eyes wide. "Why, I'm a little ol' surg'cal nurse, boss. Ah goes to work at 'leven an' gets off at seven—sometimes." A smirk accompanied her final words, "Anyone'll tell you, ah'm the Best."

Patty made a strangling sound, glanced at her watch and leaped up. "Steak for supper, people. Let's go." One by one the others stood, with the graceful Nancy lingering to walk beside Jonica while the others linked arms and started toward the dining room.

"Don't let Lindsey's joking fool you. She's a crack nurse and will back you up completely. Underneath that red hair is a dedicated Christian and a real professional."

"How old is she?" Jonica asked.

"They're all about twenty-three, just long enough out of training to remember all of what they have learned with some experience. They all did some affiliation work here and couldn't wait to apply for jobs when they became accredited." A little frown brought her silky eyebrows together. "We have a high turnover on the nursing staff, unfortunately."

Jonica stopped short and stared at her companion. She brushed away an overly friendly bee who headed for the nearest rosebush.

"I'd have thought you wouldn't have much turnover at all. Who in their right mind would want to leave all this?"

"Don't sound so disappointed." Nancy's gaze followed Jonica's around their beautiful surroundings. "It's just that we get such high quality nurses and doctors, they often end up married and deciding to go into the mission field!" Laughter filled her dark eyes. "It's a professional hazard."

Jonica bit her tongue to keep from blurting out, "Have you found it so?" but something in Nancy's natural dignity prevented it. Instead she said, "I'll have to watch my step."

"Why?" Nancy looked honestly surprised. "Believe me, if you fall in love at Shepherd of Love Hospital you know you'll have a head start on beating the divorce statistics."

"It almost sounds as if everyone here is an angel or something."

"No, Jonica. We're all sinners, but we've been saved by the grace of our Lord Jesus Christ." Nancy turned and gazed over the blue, blue Sound. "We make mistakes but we know we are forgiven so we pick ourselves up and go on. With Jesus as a Best Friend, how wrong can we get, as long as we cling close to Him and follow the path He laid out by walking it before us?"

Jonica didn't answer the rhetorical question but something inside her quivered. She'd never heard anyone talk like this, not even the ministers in the rather formal church she had made a point of attending. Her baptism had been a meaningless rite, performed because other members of her class were to join the church and she'd hoped it might make a difference. At thirteen she'd also hoped to be one of the group by conforming. Neither thing had happened but she had noticed the only really happy couples she knew were those at church. Her young heart, so deprived of love, warmth, and respect at home, silently reached out and she promised herself that one day she would find love. In a childish prayer she told God, although He had not come closer when the drops of water fell on her head, "Please, help me someday find the kindest man in the whole world, someone who will be good to me—always."

Later, she added the fruits of her observations and reached two conclusions: if she were ever to have what she called a "happily-ever-after," a hangover from fairy tale days, she must (1) find a Christian and (2) marry a professional person so her home would not be the battlefield over money her childhood home had been, with its endless wrong-side-of-the-street arguments that still assaulted her ears.

The day after the almost-date fiasco, fifteen-year-old Jonica slipped from the world she hated, willing to endure whatever it took to achieve her goals and find joy. She coolly chose nursing not from any desire to help others, although it did come later, but as an entrance into respectability and professionalism. She ignored statistics that the chance of a nurse marrying a doctor was greatly exaggerated in novels.

She would make herself so indispensable that some doctor or administrator could not help seeing her value. Unaware how deeply the fantasy had ingrained itself into her, Jonica did realize her shining knight did not ride horseback, but instead wore a stethoscope in many of her dreams.

While working in the Tacoma hospital, she had achieved the respect she sought. There had even been interns and residents who invited her out, never suspecting her outward sophistication masked insecurity and a lack of social ease. Jonica tired of them when they expected a return on their invitations at the end of the evening and so she earned a reputation for coldness. Now Nancy's blunt admission that Christians struggled but could overcome through Christ interested her. She opened her mouth to ask more, but hastily snapped it shut. As a professed Christian, she was expected to know this. She could not betray how shallow her Christianity really was and risk losing her job and the chance to live in this new world.

All through the years, Jonica had held fast to the belief that those who kept quiet and observed could learn what was necessary in almost every case. She would do the same now.

Patty, Shina, and Lindsey had already entered the dining room and taken a table when Nancy and Jonica arrived. The new nurse liked the way tables for eight stood scattered throughout the relaxing green-painted room with soft white curtains blowing in the summer breeze. "Over here," the pert blond called and Nancy led the way, explaining no special seating arrangements prevailed.

"You'll see the hospital director eating with the ward clerks, the chaplain sitting with the cleaning crew," she explained. Two young doctors proved the point by dropping into chairs at the nurses' table, then an older man approached them. "May I sit with you?"

"Of course." The table's occupants welcomed the older man with cries of delight. Jonica looked into his blue eyes and smiled. "As you said, we did meet again."

"Oh, you already know Mr. Fairchild?" Lindsey asked.

He appeared not to hear and asked one of the doctors to offer a blessing for their table. It gave the usually unshakable Jonica a chance to control herself. She barely heard the words of the blessing. If anyone had told her she would eat her first on-the-job supper at the same table with a living legend, she'd have considered that person crazy.

two

Jonica ate her delicious steak, tossed green salad and baked potato, her attention fixed on Nicholas Fairchild. How could such a great man look so humble? With a flash of insight she decided, "That's why he is so great. He sees himself as a tool in the hands of the Great Physician, of no more use on his own than a shining steel scalpel before a skilled surgeon picks it up."

Despite her lack of intimacy with a God who guided people, Jonica had been tremendously impressed by Fairchild's story, learned first from newscasts and the papers while she was still in training. Along with the rest of Seattle she had curiously watched "Fairchild's Folly" become reality, and secretly rejoiced when it happened. Watching any person do what others said couldn't be done inspired her to believe her own dreams could one day come true if she only worked hard enough.

"Mr. Fairchild." She spoke into a small pool of silence that had fallen while hungry nurses and doctors devoured the excellent meal. "Did you ever once doubt?" She thought of times when even her strongest faith faltered.

Nicholas laid down his fork and a faint flush dyed his youthful-looking skin, lightly tanned and healthy.

"I can honestly say I never doubted the existence of Shepherd of Love Hospital. Perhaps because again and again legalities and stumbling blocks disappeared." His blue eyes darkened and Jonica saw the loving way his glance traveled around the pleasant room, resting for a moment on each table filled with laughing, chatting staff members. "On the other hand, I many times wondered why God had so graciously chosen me to help accomplish what we have here today."

Jonica felt her throat constrict. Longing surged through her. How wonderful it would be to have the tranquillity she saw stamped on this man's humble face. Well, she could think of no other place on earth more inclined to foster such peace and faith than Shepherd of Love. Just a few hours at the hospital complex had clearly shown an availability of spiritual strength as well as physical healing. Such an atmosphere offered the hope that one day her own deep scars would truly mend, not just be covered up by the determination to forget.

"There's Dr. Hamilton."

Caught by a note of awe in Patty's voice that hadn't been there even for Nicholas Fairchild, Jonica amusedly looked at the blond nurse. Hero worship and deep respect shone in her eyes. Jonica suddenly felt years older than Patty or Lindsey, although so few years separated them in age. Not so with Nancy. A slight sadness when her lovely dark face wasn't smiling betrayed maturity and an evident overcoming of whatever life had handed out. And Shina remained an unknown personality.

For the second time, Patty interrupted her musings. She tackled her strawberry shortcake and laughingly confessed, "I've never wanted to work anywhere except Outpatient but if anything could lure me away, it would be that man."

"Don't talk with your mouth full," Lindsey told her.

"Yes, Mama." Patty wrinkled her tiptilted nose and swallowed before she continued. "Every single woman here admires him." She smirked at Lindsey. "Of course, since you work with him all the time you have the *best* chance. Get it?"

A mutual groan swept around the table. "Shhh," Patty warned. "He's coming over here. He probably saw Jonica."

The new nurse refused to turn and satisfy her curiosity, even when a pleasant voice spoke from behind her. "Good evening. Is this Miss Carr? Jonica?"

"Indeed it is," Mr. Fairchild said heartily. "I'd like you to meet Dr. Paul Hamilton, Miss Carr. He's our chief surgeon."

The new arrival stepped into view and held out a beautifully-shaped hand. Jonica noted the long, surgeon's fingers first, then her gaze traveled past sharply-creased gray slacks trimly belted, an open-necked white sport shirt and strong shoulders to a face neither pretty boy nor hunk—just masculine and attractive. Eyes dark as his crow-black, short hair smiled, as did firm lips. Thirty-two, perhaps, about 6'2", 200 pounds with not an ounce of fat, Jonica decided. She liked his firm handshake.

"May I?" He didn't wait for an answer but took an empty chair from a nearby table and pushed it in-between Jonica and Nancy.

"Have you had you supper, Paul?" Nicholas asked, eyes bright with approval of his chief surgeon. "He lives with his father a short distance from here," the hospital founder explained for Jonica's benefit.

"I ate with Dad but it's been all of an hour ago and we didn't have strawberry shortcake." He eyed Patty's rapidly dwindling dessert then pushed back and strode toward the kitchen. "Hope they have some left." A few moments later he returned, triumphantly smiling and carrying a huge wedge of shortcake. Jonica thought he looked like an eager boy when he dived into it. Conversation flowed around her and she relaxed. With Patty and Lindsey heckling each other and the two young doctors vying for their attention, she could relax and listen.

"Just because she's my roommate Lindsey thinks she can oversee my life." Patty gave a mock groan, then ruined the effect by adding, "I'll have to admit she does a pretty good job!"

Everyone roared, but redheaded Lindsey merely raised one eyebrow and superciliously announced, "I'm at least a month older than Patty and the Bible says we're to respect our elders."

Jonica couldn't help seeing how much Mr. Fairchild liked the good-natured ribbing. His blue eyes twinkled and, when he at last rose to go, he seemed reluctant but said he had a meeting. "I'll see you in our little prayer service before you go on duty," he told Jonica and walked away, spare frame erect.

"It's hard to believe he's seventy." Nancy Galbraith had remained quiet during the roommates' sham squabble as had Shina, who softly put in, "He's really ageless."

The doctors also excused themselves and Paul Hamilton said, "Thanks for the good company. Sorry I wasn't here the day you interviewed, Miss Carr, but

I've read your credentials and I know you'll be a tremendous asset to our surgical staff." He strode off in a long lope.

"Wow!" Patty stared after him. "I never knew him to say anything like that before."

"You mean he doesn't compliment people?" Jonica felt torn between pride and apprehension. Was the Chief Surgeon hard to work with?

"Sure he does." Lindsey scowled at her best friend. "He just usually doesn't make it quite so strong." A smile of pure mischief turned her freckles to tiny copper pennies. "Looks like someone has finally made an impression on our good doctor."

"It's about time," Patty began, but Lindsey and Shina shushed her and the five nurses left the dining hall, saying, "Come on, Jonica—we can call you that, can't we? Last names are so impersonal." Jonica nodded and Patty said, "We'll show you our rooms. Shina lives with her family and drives in, though."

She led the way to the T-shaped building that housed staff. Jonica admired its efficiency. Two stories high, the covered passageway that protected staff from bad weather opened into the middle of the lower floor in the center of the T's cross bar, a lovely living room that could have done credit to any nice home.

The east end of the cross bar held filled bookshelves that made Jonica, an avid reader, long to drop into a comfortable chair and take time to indulge herself.

"There's a library of medical books in the hospital itself," Lindsey explained. "These are the best of the current Christian and secular books available, everything from novels to Bible studies, plus a whole lot more."

"The planners deliberately put the library on this side of the living room so it would be quiet," Shina said. "There's a recreation room with TV, piano, tape players, pingpong table, and games on the west side, with a small laundry room on the end, although the hospital laundry will do our uniforms."

Jonica already knew the upright of the T contained eleven rooms downstairs, eleven up: five on each side of the hall and one longer, narrower at the end.

"Men upstairs, women down," Nancy explained. "I'm right next to you." She flung open the door of a charming suite done in rose and white. "Patty and Lindsey's is a double and bigger, two doors down."

Jonica admired the soft greens but privately considered her room the prettiest. She flushed and asked, "I have a better view—why didn't one of you take that room when it became available?"

"We all live in the ones we have since first coming to Shepherd of Love," Patty explained, suddenly serious. "The personnel division asked if we wished to change and we said no. So did the other women." She smiled a singularly sweet smile. "Besides, we heard you were coming so we saved the room for you. We're hoping you'll want to stay a long time."

A rush of emotion threatened to swamp Jonica. She had never lived with a group of women who saved the best for a stranger. On the contrary, through college and afterwards, she as well as her colleagues went for what they wanted. *I'm going to have a lot to learn in order to fit in*, she realized. "How many other staff members live here?"

"It varies," Shina said. "If my family didn't want me to stay at home so badly I'd love to live here. I'm working on it. My favorite is the yellow room you could have chosen, right down here next to all of you. I think I'm making progress, too. Father said the other day he didn't like seeing me so tired from commuting and driving after dark when I have evening or night shifts." Her charming slanted eyes sparkled. "Maybe soon you'll have another occupant."

"All the other rooms are filled," Patty informed them. "And sometimes there's a waiting list, so if you want that room, Shina, you'd better say so quick."

The doll-like nurse smiled. "That decides it. I'll talk with Father and Mother tonight." She glanced at her watch. "Oh-oh, we'd better let Jonica finish getting settled before she goes on duty."

"You know you report a half hour early, don't you?" Nancy reminded. "Each shift starts with a short staff prayer service and reports from the previous shift."

"I won't be late."

"If you want to catch a nap, I'll rap on the door when it's fifteen minutes before you have to leave," Nancy promised.

"I don't think I'll sleep. I'm too excited."

Lindsey fired a parting shot. She drew her lanky body up to full height, perhaps an inch shorter than Jonica but slimmer.

"Nurse Carr, I must remind you that charge nurses must never get excited. They are to remain in control at all times so their subordinates, meaning slaves like me, can have a good example set before them and—" She dropped her lecturing pretense and promised to wait for her new supervisor. Again Jonica marveled at the camaraderie between employees. No abominable caste system here that distanced floor nurse from charge nurse from nurse manager.

Her attractive rooms held out welcoming arms when she stepped into her suite. Earlier she had gone out and locked the door leading outdoors. This time she came in from the long corridor, wondering about the other residents. If the nurses she had met so far were representative, living conditions couldn't help but be ideal. She dropped lightly to the comfortable couch provided as part of the furnishings. No need to open the bed in the opposite corner.

Bits and pieces flashed through her overactive mind, feelings and comments, personalities and questions. Then her training stepped forward at her command. Jonica shut off everything, blanked her mind, took deep and relaxing breaths and slept until tapping at the door and Nancy's soft, "Fifteen minute warning" brought her awake and refreshed.

By the time Jonica had slid into the pantsuit uniform she'd chosen for her first shift, Lindsey appeared wearing a similar outfit.

"I crawl into my surgical blues once on duty," she said. "But I like to have something else with me. If it isn't too rough a night, I can change there for breakfast. If it is—it's back here for a shower before I show up in the staff dining room." A lovely pink crept into her freckled cheeks. "No use looking like a drab."

Jonica suspected one of the young doctors who had joined them for supper might have something to do with Lindsey's elaborate explanation but said nothing. Not until a firmer foundation had been established would she make observations that could be construed as prying. She changed the subject.

"Have you had a lot of rough nights lately?"

"No, but it's just when things are going well that something can happen, pray God it doesn't." She sobered and a look of pain came into her brown eyes. "One of the nurses I trained with works at Harborview. I admire her but I couldn't handle her job. Harborview has a terrific trauma unit and gets some horrendous cases—bad burns flown in by helicopter, victims of gang fights; that kind of thing. We send our most critically injured to them. Shepherd of Love is a wonderful hospital but it can't be all things to all people so we work closely with the other Seattle hospitals."

"Is there any problem of feeling too proud to ask for help?"

Lindsey's eyes rounded. "Of course not. We want the very best for every single person who walks or is carried in our doors. When we can't give it, we send patients to someone who can—although it's really Someone with a capital S who holds the ultimate outcome in His hands."

"You're very sure of that, aren't you." A statement, not a question, yet Jonica held her breath waiting for the reply.

"If I weren't, I wouldn't be here," Lindsey said simply. "Neither would any of the others. Take Dr. Hamilton, for example. He could work at any hospital in Seattle but he believes healing comes from God working with and through His servants so he stays here at Shepherd of Love. Although I heard a rumor—" She knitted her brows and broke off. They'd reached the end of the long covered passage and the doors to the main hospital building. "Enough gossip. We have a job to do."

Jonica knew from the time she gathered with her night shift staff in the little prayer meeting, everything in life before had pointed her to this moment. She had felt it just before entering the hospital director's office earlier that day. The feeling had intensified with her fellow nurses' friendliness. Now, while one of the chaplains conducted a very brief service in which critically ill and recuperating patients alike were brought before the Lord to receive the blessing they most needed, Jonica let the wonder sink into her soul. She rose with the rest, strengthened and ready. Yet she lingered a moment to shyly ask the chaplain, "Do the patients know we pray for them?"

"Yes, Miss Carr. And the amazing thing is, even those who profess to have no belief in God never object. I've heard self-proclaimed atheists mutter, 'can't do no harm' and go under the anesthetic far more relaxed than they realize."

Jonica slipped away, still marveling.

Once she met the rest of her night shift, any remaining qualm about efficiency died forever. She also learned that her department did not begin and end with the arrival and departure of patients, but carried over into other parts of the hospital When sent to ICU* they still continued as part of the surgical team's concern. They remained on Surgery's prayer list while on the wards and until released from the hospital or into the Heavenly Father's justice and mercy. So did their loved ones who

*intensive care unit

experienced a different type of pain, often even deeper than the patient's.

The night passed quietly. The sterile instruments and gleaming life-giving machines remained in waiting, ready when needed. Halfway through the shift, Jonica put Emily, a fiftyish surgical nurse with the most seniority, in charge while she took a break. When Lindsey introduced Emily, the new charge nurse looked at her keenly, wondering if there would be any resentment from having to take orders from someone not even half her age. One look into the steady gray eyes dispelled that fear. So did Emily's comment, "Dr. Hamilton's already told me how blessed we are to have you here."

Pleasure sent a little red flag of color to Jonica's face. "That will give me something to live up to, Emily."

"Don't worry about it. No one here has. God's not about to send some flibbertigibbet after all the praying we did for just the right person." She smiled and motioned her supervisor away. "We'll page you if you're needed. Take your break." The telephone rang. Jonica paused. Emily answered, quickly handing it to her.

"Emergency. We're sending up a male Caucasian . . . ." In staccato sentences, the ER gave the vital statistics. Jonica repeated them for Emily and Lindsey's benefit, pen racing. Before she completed the call her trustworthy two had flown to scrub.

"Who's on call?" Jonica desperately wished she knew every surgeon personally. What appeared to be a ruptured appendix would require skill, speed and teamwork.

"Dr. Hamilton." Lindsey continued to scrub hands and arms while she answered. "Will you assist?"

"Yes." Jonica hurried to get scrubbed. "Emily, circulate. Lindsey, double-check the instrument table."

Even before the patient appeared, Dr. Hamilton loped in, glanced at the meticulous arrangements and nodded approval. "Glad to have you aboard, Jonica. Emily, Lindsey, this is old stuff for us." Gowned, masked and ready they nodded. The surgeon scrubbed and stood alert. "Good thing I dropped in to see how one of my patients was making it," he said from behind his sterile mask. He sighed and Jonica saw the brooding look in his dark eyes above the gauze.

"ER filled me in a bit more. Man had been having pains all day, thought he had a virus. Took antacid and it didn't help. Temperature rose and scared his wife. Patient didn't want to come because it had stopped hurting. He's probably filled with infection. Let's pray before he gets here."

Never had Jonica experienced anything stranger than standing in that operating room ready to assist with surgery and listening to the surgeon pray for the patient, the staff and himself.

The same skill that earned her the job bonded her into the surgical team. She slapped instruments into Paul Hamilton's hand as if they had worked together for years, anticipating his needs. Only once did he have to ask for a particular instrument. Like a miracle of life, the pallid face of the patient tinged with color and Jonica rejoiced. She also remembered to whisper a prayer of thanks, although her lips twisted wryly and she wondered if she did it because like the atheist said, 'it can't do no harm,' or if she really believed God, not Dr. Paul Hamilton, had saved the man.

"If antibiotics do their job, he should live for many years," the doctor announced when they had finished and were cleaning up. "Thanks, team." He smiled at each in exactly the same way, from hastily summoned anesthetist to the cleaning crew waiting to restore the operating room to sterility and perfect order, then walked out with a spring in his step.

"Does he always walk that way?" Jonica didn't realize she'd spoken aloud until Lindsey soberly said, "Only when he feels the patient will recover." She dried her hands, grimaced and added, "I want a shower before breakfast but you have to give your report to the day shift so I'll see you in a bit." A brilliant smile tilted her mobile lips upward. "You did great, boss." She disappeared out the door, but her warm approval stayed behind like a summer day's lingering warmth after the sun set over Puget Sound.

three

Dr. Paul Hamilton flicked the remote control. The garage door of the home he'd lived in as long as he could remember slid open. He drove his Honda Accord in, shut off the motor and got out, pausing to listen to the singing of a bird choir in a nearby maple. Exhilarated by the way the surgery had gone, he smiled at the dawning sky and said, "Thank you, Lord" before closing the garage door and fitting his key into the kitchen door lock.

"It's unlocked, son," a resonant voice called.

Paul pushed the door wide. "Dad, how many times have I told you not to wait up for me?"

"I didn't." Innocence wreathed the lean face that resembled Paul's, except prematurely snow-white hair crowned Peter Hamilton's young-looking face. "I heard you leave and decided it was a good time for prayer."

A look of warm understanding and mutual respect flowed between them and Paul flinched, wondering how Dad would react if one day his only son decided to follow his heart. He quickly clamped down on the thought. Right now, his future remained nebulous and certain dreams unpredictable. He sniffed. "Bacon and eggs?"

"Plus orange juice, hot muffins and jam in ten minutes; just enough time for you to change." Peter slipped the pan of muffins into the conventional oven, scorning the microwave Paul favored when he infrequently cooked.

44

"How do you always know the exact time to have meals ready?" Paul demanded.

"The Lord works in mysterious ways." The older man expertly turned the bacon and turned the burner to low.

Paul chuckled all the way to the shower off his bedroom. Leave it to Dad to come up with that kind of answer! Yet, was it so strange? From the day Dr. Peter Hamilton gathered his small son close in his arms and said, "Mother's gone to live with Jesus, son, but we have each other. It's going to be lonely and we'll miss her, but she won't have to be sick ever again. Someday, after we've done the work here on earth God has for us to accomplish, we'll go live with her forever," a far closer bond than father-son existed between the two. They kept their wife and mother alive through photos and memories, and always the hope for a glorious tomorrow.

As Paul grew and made childhood friends, then older companions, no one ever replaced his father as number one. All the old-fashioned words that described such a friendship as theirs—buddy or pal—fell short. Yet Dr. Peter, as his colleagues knew him, refrained from telling his son what to do. When Paul brought his troubles and choices to him, Peter wisely discussed all the options and their possible results, then trusted the solid foundation he had built in the boy's life for the right decision. A few times Paul chose less than best but with his clear vision and prompted by, "What would Dad and Mom and God want me to do?" he soon corrected things.

Now Paul toweled himself vigorously, donned casual clothes and brushed his short, wet hair. He thought of the moment he'd told Dad he planned to follow in his steps. For only the second time in his life, Paul saw his father cry. Only this time the tears signified joy, not the loss of a beloved, faithful wife.

Sudden depression blighted Paul's mood. Perhaps the stirrings inside him, the discontent, meant he simply needed a vacation. Somehow, there never seemed to be a good time. Always a special patient—and every patient became special to him—needed his skill. He wasn't arrogant enough to believe no one else could care for those persons; he simply grew into the lives of all who sought him and humbly gave his best.

"Wonder how Dad would like to go fishing?" he mused, then headed for the kitchen and breakfast.

How many times had he and Dad sat at the small table next to the bay window overlooking Mt. Rainier, sharing ideas, and cases and the goodness of their Master? Simple white curtains, a replica of those that had hung there before Mrs. Hamilton died, were pulled back and framed a magnificent view of the still-snowcapped peak.

After the blessing, Paul loaded his plate with everything in sight. Peter stuck with the muffins and juice. Since his mild stroke that necessitated an extended leave of absence from his practice, he faithfully avoided cholesterol-high foods. So did Paul, for the most part. His father had become an excellent cook and planned healthful, attractive meals. Only occasionally did he serve bacon or eggs.

Pride rested in his black eyes and he abruptly said, "You know, son, all these years of living together we've only had one serious disagreement. I call that remarkable."

His comment followed so closely along the lines Paul

had been thinking that he laid down his fork. "Lacy."

"Yes." Dr. Peter cocked one eyebrow in the same mannerism he so often used. "She's back in Seattle."

"Really? I couldn't care less." Paul resumed eating and his heart didn't skip a single beat.

"There was a time. . ."

Paul grimly supplied the missing words. "When I was a total fool. Thank God I didn't wreck my life and that He showed me her false nature before we married."

Dr. Peter's face wore a troubled expression. "She's getting a divorce." He hesitated. "Now that you've earned status as a surgeon, Mrs. Jones-Duncan, as I understand she wishes to be known, may find you—attractive."

Paul set down his juice glass. "I hope she doesn't. I have absolutely no feelings for Lacy, not even anger." He tilted his chair back, folded his hands behind his head and stared unseeingly at Mt. Rainier, which had turned strawberry-ice-cream pink from the rising sun.

"Psychologists say people always remember their first loves. I guess puppy love describes my experience, or infatuation. A seventeen-year-old boy is dazzled by a tiny, blond cheerleader. They pledge mutual love and think it will last forever. Graduation means a step closer to marriage to her, a step closer to becoming a doctor to the boy who is leaving childhood behind and becoming a man. Bitter arguments and tears follow, accusations that he doesn't love her or he wouldn't forget her while preparing for a profession that takes forever. An older, richer fish swims into her social pool. Girl leaves boy, marries for money. Boy grieves. God opens his eyes and the day comes when the boy, a man now, forgives her and finds in doing so, he is free."

"Well said, son." Dr. Peter sounded relieved. "I appreciate your opening your heart. You're right—no one can ever be a truly free person until he forgives those who have wronged him."

Paul put his chair back on all four legs and picked up his fork again.

"You always knew how shallow Lacy really was, didn't you? I know you kept still when I raved about her but I could tell you didn't agree with my estimate, especially when I considered her an angel sent from heaven just for me. Funny how we twist what we want into believing it's what God wants for us. You're right, though. Lacy is about the only thing we've disagreed on."

"The New Testament Peter and Paul had their differences too," Dr. Peter reminded his son and they both laughed. Paul had known from babyhood his mother chose the name Paul after the grand old warhorse in the Bible who carried the gospel to many in his lifetime and to countless millions after his death through his epistles. Small he might have been, but tall he stood in the history of the earth. A name to be proud of, one that needed his namesake's best.

Filled with good food, that namesake yawned and stretched. "I'm hitting the sack. I'm scheduled for gall bladder surgery at two. Oh, Dad, the new night charge nurse came and she's a wonder. Never saw anyone better at anticipating what I needed and getting it to me." Admiration gave way to a frown. "I think we need to keep her in our prayers, though."

"Why?" Dr. Peter leaned forward, interested and ready.

"I don't exactly know. Something in her eyes. I got

the feeling she hasn't had the happiest life in the world.
She has blue eyes but at times they darken until they
almost look black."

"You noticed all that during surgery? My, you are ob-
servant," Dr. Peter said mildly.

Paul laughed, yawned again. "I met her at supper.
We were too busy cleaning up a ruptured appendix later
to get much of a look."

"What's she like? I had a chat with Nicholas Fairchild
after Miss—Carr, isn't it—interviewed. He said if her
recommendations are to be believed, she's a whiz; his
word, not mine. It's probably out of date now."

"Maybe, but it describes her." Weariness forgotten
for a moment, Paul added, "I'll admit I wondered how
any woman that young could be a charge nurse, even
on night shift. Her records half-convinced me and
tonight's performance won me completely. She's
going to be one of the best things that's happened to
Shepherd of Love for a long time, although all our staff
is top-notch." He stood, stretched until his fingertips
grazed the ceiling and headed toward the hall that led to
the bedroom area. "What's she like? Tall, I'd guess
about 5'10". Strong—145 lbs., maybe more, but perfectly proportioned. Surprisingly slim hands. Carries
her head up, her shoulders back. Eyes front like a sol-
dier facing a hostile area. Plain brown hair and no
makeup I could see except lipstick. Not a bit pretty, but
an interesting face with smooth skin."

If Dr. Peter secretly wondered at the detailed
description of the newcomer, he kept it to himself.
"Doesn't sound much like Lacy."

Paul laughed until the house filled with his mirth.

"Wait until you see Jonica and you'll see how right you are!"

"She's a Christian, of course, or she wouldn't be working at Shepherd of Love." Dr. Peter stacked the dishes.

"You said it." This time the yawn threatened to dislocate Paul's jaw. "Call me at twelve-thirty, Dad." He whistled a few bars of "Surely Goodness and Mercy" and went to a well-deserved, much-needed rest.

The inner alarm that seldom failed him roused Paul from a deep sleep just five minutes before time to be called. Before Dr. Peter knocked on his door, he was up and dressed, his mind busy with the upcoming surgery. In spite of the enormous early breakfast, he did full justice to lunch: homemade vegetable soup with good bread and a vegetable and fresh fruit tray. He also discussed the surgery just ahead and the two doctors joined in prayer.

The short drive to the hospital offered summer at its best. The fragrance of freshly-mowed lawns, nodding roses and a tang of salt from the Sound came through the open car window. A verse from James Russell Lowell's poem "June" from *The Vision of Sir Launfal*, learned at his father's knee, came to mind and Paul softly quoted:

> *And what is so rare as a day in June?*
> *Then, if ever, come perfect days;*
> *Then Heaven tries earth if it be in tune,*
> *And over it softly her warm ear lays;*
> *Whether we look, or whether we listen,*
> *We hear life murmur, or see it glisten.*

Nothing could be more true in Seattle. Spring rains that gave way to days like this made them even more appreciated than places that boasted continuous sunshine and flowers. Once at the hospital, Paul parked and walked inside, only then remembering he'd forgotten to ask Dad about going fishing. He shrugged. Time enough for that once he finished his day's work.

The gall bladder removal went even better than the early morning surgery, yet Paul noticed a difference. His assisting doctor and nurse, anesthetist and others were just as competent, yet he vaguely missed Jonica Carr's deft skill, her confident selection of the instruments he would need next. The male nurse who performed today's work did a fine job but not quite so rapidly. He waited to be asked rather than intuitively sensing the surgeon's needs.

"Go ahead and close," Paul told his assistant surgeon, then stepped back and observed. Any time he felt comfortable doing so, he allowed his assistant to gain valuable experience. Unlike some surgeons, however, he never left the operating room until the final suture had been set and the bandaging done. It had nothing to do with trust. He would gladly go under the knife of any surgeon who practiced at Shepherd of Love. He simply always remembered his father's advice, "Never leave any task until it is completed," and lived by that rule except in the rare instances when summoned to the second operating room in case of emergency.

Paul decided to use the free time period following surgery to catch up on some reading. A stack of new medical journals in the doctors' lounge offered interesting developments. He considered it part of his stewardship to keep informed. Science and medicine continued to make such giant strides no physician or surgeon dared to stop studying. In addition, the comfortable room held easy chairs and off-duty personnel frequented it.

Today it lay empty with sunlight streaming through the natural woven blinds lowered to filter it because of the western exposure. Paul idly scanned article titles, dipping into those that interested him most. He sighed when he heard himself paged. "Dr. Hamilton, please report to the Central Waiting Area." Long strides took him down the corridor past Radiology and the Lab, the Surgicenter suite, and ICU. He turned sharply and reached the open area in the center of the lower floor, with it airy feeling enhanced by a large skylight and off-white tile. Attractive couches and chairs flanked magazine stands. An information desk stood at one side, but before he reached it, a petite, blond whirlwind met him.

"Hello, Paul."

For a fraction of a second he was seventeen again, swelling with pride that his girl was the prettiest girl in school. A heartbeat later he rejoiced. Not a flutter of pulse accompanied his first look into Lacy Jones-Duncan's pert face after thirteen years, only sadness when his sharp gaze picked out tiny lines beneath the carefully applied makeup, a quickly hidden tightening of her thin lips. She didn't look thirty-two; neither was she the high school cheerleader he'd fallen for like a load of rock being dumped, in spite of her unchanged figure. "Hello, Lacy. Dad said he heard you were back."

She offered her hand. He took it, uncomfortable when

the small, soft fingers curled around his and she said in a husky voice, "You haven't changed, except now you're a man."

He shook off her clinging grip, seated her on a couch and took the chair at the end, despite her motioning for him to sit next to her. Her next words shocked him.

"Have you changed, Paul? Inside, I mean? I know you never married. It's one of the reasons I—" She looked down then swept him an upward glance. He recognized it as the same appeal for sympathy she used to win from his boyish heart—the determination to protect and fight for her long after the days of chivalry ended.

How could he ever have been deceived? Paul crossed his arms and looked straight into her brimming blue eyes from which not a single tear fell to mar her makeup. "I am sorry to hear you are leaving your husband, Lacy."

"Are you?" She clasped her hands as if in prayer. Disappointment filled her face. "If you only knew how much I regretted my marriage. I was selfish and wanted my own way. Before I'd been married six months, I knew what an awful thing it was to marry a man I didn't love, could never love. All these years, I can't tell you what it's been like. I stayed with him but I never forgot you. Darling, have you forgiven me?"

"Long ago, Lacy," he told her honestly.

"Then everything will be all right." She held out a white hand free of rings. "We can pick up right where we left off when I insanely listened to—"

Paul got up and stared at her. "Never."

She also rose. "But you said you'd forgiven me."

Aware of curious stares from various staff members

and visitors, Paul lowered his voice. "I have absolutely no feelings for you, angry or otherwise. I'm sorry you aren't happy but it has nothing to do with me."

"It has everything to do with you. I left my husband for you and told him so." Her face hardened, then melted.

He couldn't believe the rage that filled him. To keep from saying things that would dishonor his Lord, Paul chilled his voice and merely stated, "That is highly unfortunate, Mrs. Duncan, but I am not responsible for your actions."

He loped off, feeling her angry gaze boring into his back. Unable to get the disturbing scene out of his mind, he went back and checked the surgical schedule. Nothing for him until the next morning and another surgeon on call. Good. He needed to get away—from the hospital, from anything that would remind him of Lacy Jones-Duncan standing in the Central Waiting Area and calmly disclosing she had left her husband—for him! Could anything be more grotesque? He felt unclean from the encounter. He, who hated divorce, although realized it was necessary in rare cases. He, who had kept himself physically, morally and mentally free of temptation. His close relationship with God permitted no dallying with impure thoughts that could lead to sin. If ever he married, he would bring to his bride a clean slate and expected to receive the same. He despised the current trend of labeling immorality "natural," to be indulged in at will. His Bible told him differently. While he did not condemn those who slipped, and repeatedly told them God offered forgiveness for all sin, he shrank from becoming even temporarily separated from God by his own actions.

"Now is a good time to go fishing," he murmured. "We can head out right away, get in a few hours and have time to talk. Doesn't matter if we catch anything or not."

Dr. Peter agreed and they headed for a stream east of Bellevue, far enough off the beaten path that it hadn't been infested with fishermen. It required a three-mile climb to reach it and by the time they got there, much of Paul's disgust had been worked out in the steep terrain. In addition, his father's quiet, "Leave it in God's hands," had stilled the tumult, as it always did. They caught no fish, but neither cared.

"No man ever had a better dad," Paul said on the way home, hands steady on the wheel. "I noticed you did splendidly on the hike, too. Before long you'll be back practicing."

"I can hardly wait." Dr. Peter stared at the darkening evening. "But you'll lose a mighty fine cook." His voice sounded husky. "Paul, if your mother knows how you turned out, and I can't help believing she does, I know she's just as proud as I am."

"Thanks, Dad." He cleared his throat of the sudden obstruction that rose at the tribute and they finished the rest of the drive in the silence of companionship that has no need for words.

four

Jonica slept deeply and dreamlessly after her first night on duty at Shepherd of Love. When she awakened in mid-afternoon, she decided to put her kitchenette to use and prepared a light meal, just enough to keep her going until supper. Several in-between hours loomed before she had to go on duty again, so she decided to wander through the hospital complex and familiarize herself with the location of the various departments. The day she had interviewed, the relaxed but efficient atmosphere had made a good impression but she had been mainly concerned with how her interview went. She also had to hurry back to Tacoma and her next shift. Now she could take the time to simply prowl and observe.

A curving staircase rose from the Central Waiting Area to the second floor. Jonica admired the skylighted area and contrasted it with some of the stuffy waiting rooms she had seen. Her sharp gaze noted the abundance of books and magazines provided and the high percentage of Christian reading material and Bibles. Already she felt part of the hospital team and she made a point of smiling at staff, patients and visitors.

The Family Center, which included Parenting Education, Labor and Delivery, Recovery, Pediatrics and Children's Therapy, occupied one entire side of the second story. Nancy Galbraith, busy with her small charges in Pediatrics, waved and called, "Feel free," then gestured around the colorfully decorated ward and semi-private rooms. Jonica caught a glimpse of doll-like Shina Ito hurrying toward a delivery room. Neither nurse wore traditional white. Nancy explained Nicholas Fairchild felt pastel uniforms offered brightness to sick children's lives and the nurses were only too glad to choose pink, blue, green, yellow, or peach in place of stark white.

The opposite side of the building housed Oncology, and Occupational and Physical Therapy. Through shining windows she glimpsed the single story Retirement Center, reached by a covered passage but partially screened off by trees to give residents the same privacy the staff enjoyed in their quarters.

Not an inch of space had been wasted in the designing of the complex yet a feeling of spaciousness pervaded. Linen and storage closets filled nooks between departments. Adequate lounges offered the staff a comfortable place to rest. A solarium tucked away at one end hosted disabled patients and a multitude of green, growing things, as well as fresh air and sunlight.

Jonica marveled at the completeness of the small hospital. She slowly retraced her steps to the staircase leading down to the Central Waiting Area and descended. Halfway down she stopped abruptly. For the moment, she had the stairway to herself, but below her and a little to one side Dr. Paul Hamilton stood talking with a petite blond woman. Caught in the uncomfortable position of eavesdropper to the conversation that rose with the small woman's voice, Jonica hesitated. If she turned and went back upstairs, surely the two would see her. She could avert her gaze and go down, yet that meant they would also know she had heard their conversation. She stood quietly, wishing herself anywhere but there, while the woman in the too-young outfit brazenly proclaimed an undying love for the stern-faced doctor who stood staring at her. Several staff members and visitors had come into the open space and Jonica caught their curious glances.

Couldn't the woman see them? Or didn't she care? Her angry voice floated up to where Jonica tried to make herself inconspicuous, despising the stranger for the humiliation she was obviously causing Jonica's new boss.

"I left my husband for you and told him so." The blond made no effort to lower her voice.

Paul Hamilton's reply came as clear as if produced in a sound chamber.

"That is highly unfortunate, Mrs. Duncan, but I am not responsible for your actions."

"Bravo," Jonica inwardly shouted and a little smile played on her lips. Dr. Hamilton's abrupt departure released the new nurse from her unwilling role as listener. She took a few steps downward but stopped again at the look that filled the woman's face. The blond's features contorted in a combination of chagrin, anger and spite until Jonica shivered. All the expensive garb in the world—and the blond wore as costly an outfit as Jonica had ever seen—didn't hide the same look of vindictiveness Jonica had faced a thousand times before: from her stepfather and from all those who live to get even with someone for an insult real or imagined.

She couldn't tear her gaze away from the woman.

Perhaps the visitor felt it. She glanced up. Blue eyes colder than surgical steel swept Jonica's tall frame. She marched toward the stairway and rudely demanded, "Just why are you staring at me?"

Feeling as put down as she had all through high school when her strong build contrasted with the tiny girls, who scooped up the boys' hearts and all the honors except those Jonica claimed, the dignity of her profession braced Jonica. She didn't reply. Instead, she simply walked down to the Central Waiting Area, brushed past the woman as if she didn't exist and walked away, head high. Yet she couldn't help wondering how this unpleasant person had touched Dr. Hamilton's life. Obviously there had once been something between them.

"Psst. Jonica." A flushed face and beckoning hand motioned her from behind a screen of living green that partitioned off a small space. "Mercy, did you get a load of Her Nibs?" Patty Thompson's innocent blue eyes had rounded to saucer-like proportions.

"How could I help it? Her voice certainly carried." Jonica let out an exasperated breath. "Who is she, anyway?"

"The Queen of Sheba. Well, almost." Patty giggled but fierce resentment showed in her pretty face and the newcomer again felt the bonds of loyalty that existed at Shepherd of Love for one of its own against anyone who dared attack a staff member, verbally or otherwise. "About a million years ago, right out of high school, Lacy Jones, Jones-Duncan now, pressed for Dr. Hamilton to marry her."

"They were sweethearts?" Jonica found the

idea distasteful.

"High school stuff. You know, cheerleader dazzlement," Patty grimaced. "That's probably not a word but it describes it." She rushed on. "He said no way, according to rumor. She married pots of money and now she's back." Shrewd knowledge of human nature touched Patty's face. "He's big game, now. She's already got the money but Duncan's a jerk, drinks a lot." She shrugged and looked ashamed. "Guess I shouldn't judge. If I had to be married to someone like her, I might not be any better."

"So here she is trying to rekindle an old flame."

"She won't." Patty drew herself up to her full five-foot-five-inch height, a small mother hen ready to do battle for Dr. Hamilton, who resembled a frail chick less than anyone in the world.

Patty glanced at her watch. "Uh-oh, I have to go. Break's over." She started off in the rapid nurse's walk that covered ground but didn't alarm patients or visitors. Then she turned. "Jonica, if I were you I'd run like crazy if I saw Ms. Lacy Jones-Duncan coming my way. When you didn't answer her question and went past her, something in her eyes. . ." Patty didn't finish. "I'm not a scaredy cat but the way she looked sent ice cubes down my spine." She walked on down the hall toward the corner that led to Outpatient, leaving Jonica standing there torn between her new friend's concern and the desire to laugh. Little likelihood existed that she'd have any dealings with the blonde bombshell who wanted an old love back.

Again the corners of her lips went up. If the chill in his voice represented his true feelings, the Chief

Surgeon at Shepherd of Love wasn't about to fall like a ripe peach at his former lady-love's feet.

Jonica's smile died. She blinked and wondered why a sudden depression had fallen like a blight over her excitement and newfound joy. Patty's warning certainly wasn't responsible. Could it be that seeing the tiny blond and learning she had once attracted the tall Dr. Hamilton brought back all her dislike of her own sturdy body? "Don't be a fool," she muttered to herself once she got outside and a little breeze off the Sound cooled her flaming cheeks. "You're here to work, not to find a man." She ignored the mocking little voice inside that taunted, *Is that so?* and kept walking. Yet her honest heart admitted that when she did find someone to love, she hoped he'd be tall, strong and caring like her new boss.

Day by day her new job absorbed her attention until the scene in the Central Waiting Area it took on a dreamlike quality. A few times she caught glimpses of Lacy Jones-Duncan pattering here and there in the hospital on ridiculously spiked heels, usually with face tilted admiringly at a tall specialist or resident—but never at Dr. Hamilton. An unspoken sympathy for the man obviously being stalked ran in currents throughout Shepherd of Love and many a ploy protected the Chief Surgeon from Lacy's continuous presence. When she had him paged, someone else appeared with the information he wasn't available.

"He isn't, to her." Red-haired, freckled Lindsey deftly set controls on the sterilizer. Little gold specks danced in her brown eyes.

"He never will be," gray-eyed Emily crisply added. "The sooner that one knows it, the better." She sighed.

"It's not in Dr. Hamilton to be downright rude but I'm beginning to think that's what he will have to do to 'get shut of her' as my grandma used to say."

Suddenly Lacy no longer haunted the hospital halls. No one knew why but Emily's eyes gleamed. Perhaps she had talked with the tall doctor. In any event, the Surgicenter breathed more easily than it had in weeks until a rainy summer night when screaming ambulances showed the toll the weather had exacted. "During dry spells road oil films the highways," Emily said. "Until enough rain falls to wash it away, it's like a coating of ice and most drivers don't recognize it. The man and woman being sent up now were traveling far too fast for the condition of the road and now they are paying for it."

The door burst open. Paul Hamilton charged in, face white.

"What is it?" Lindsey demanded.

He pressed his lips in a straight line. "Mrs. Duncan is being brought in for immediate surgery." He strode to a sink and began to scrub. "So is her husband. He's the most critical so I'll take him. Another surgeon's been called in to care for Lacy. She has deep gashes on her legs and arms but will be all right."

"I thought they were divorced," Emily put in.

"I did, too." He broke off. "Poor guy, I'd send him to Harborview if I dared but his wife—if she still is that—absolutely insisted he be cared for here. It's going to be a long hard surgery. Jonica, you'll assist me?"

"Of course." Yet in spite of her experience she had to breathe deeply when she saw their patient. She had never seen such an extensive head wound. Only God could save this man. All through the long hours, she prayed and slapped instruments into Paul's capable hands. She marveled at the way his steady fingers probed, at how his quiet voice gave instructions.

Suddenly the anesthetist barked, "Blood pressure dropping. We're losing him!"

"Steady." Dr. Hamilton's eyes glowed above his mask. "God, help us according to Your will." A succession of maneuvers followed, a trained team doing everything possible to extend life—to no avail. Duncan refused to respond to treatment. He died on the operating table despite heroic efforts on the part of the dedicated staff.

Brain dull with fatigue, Jonica stumbled out. In a few moments, she would issue orders for cleaning up, although the crew knew all too well how urgent such work was on a night that could produce many other demands for the operating theatres. Dr. Hamilton stood with shoulders slumped, staring at the wall. He turned when she came up to him. "We did our best."

"Yes." Jonica choked over the word. How futile it seemed when their best wasn't good enough. A new thought entered her weary mind. "I wonder how Mrs.—his wife—is and how she will take it."

"God help us all when we tell her." Paul's dark eyes filled with trouble. "No one on earth can predict how Lacy will react." He looked down at his stained hand and clothing. "I'd better get cleaned up, just in case."

Compassion caused Jonica to reach out a detaining hand and impulsively lay it on his sleeve. "Everyone in the O.R. knows how hard you tried."

Slowly some of the strain left his lean face. "Thank you." A look of gratitude and something Jonica could not interpret lighted his face. He touched her hand lightly then wheeled and went to get cleaned up.

Surprisingly, no more cases came up from the Emergency Room. "E.R. does a great job," Emily told the younger nurses. "Good thing, too. I have a feeling we'll have our hands full with the patient we have and she isn't even hurt badly."

The prediction proved all too accurate. Jonica had accompanied Lacy to a recovery room and lingered while a special* hovered over her. Before the patient would consent to being treated, she had demanded full anesthesia and round-the-clock specials. Lindsey and Emily were too valuable to tie up in maintenance care so a part-time special came in.

"Let me know the minute she's conscious," Jonica directed. "She has to be told about her husband."

"Better let Dr. Hamilton do that," the special suggested. "She's not likely to take the news well from a nurse."

Jonica didn't know what to expect. Lacy obviously hadn't loved Duncan but her unpredictable nature could erupt in a dozen different ways. Because of this, Jonica sent the special on break and remained out of Lacy's sight when Dr. Hamilton came in, compassion in his face.

"Lacy, I have bad news for you. We did everything we possibly could but your hus-Duncan didn't make it through surgery. Even if he had, his brain was so damaged he could never have been completely normal again."

*special duty nurse

The blue eyes showed she understood but Lacy said nothing. Jonica held her breath and waited. Dr. Hamilton stood rigid by the bed. "Do you understand what I'm saying?"

"Yes. I needn't have divorced him."

Paul straightened as if he'd been hit.

"Don't look so shocked." Lacy stretched out a hand toward him. "He wouldn't have wanted to live if he—" For the first time she seemed to think of her own injuries. "Am I going to be scarred?"

"Plastic surgery will erase almost every trace, in time." Jonica sensed cold anger beneath the commonplace words.

Lacy closed her eyes. When she opened them again she whispered, "I should never have gone with him tonight but he pleaded and I do like the Space Needle. Paul." A little color came into her face. "It's all for the best, Fate, maybe. I know you hate divorce but now we won't have to worry about it, will we?" She licked dry lips and it reminded Jonica of a sleek cat getting into cream.

"You don't know what you're saying, Mrs. Duncan. Now I suggest that you rest." He turned to go.

"I do know what I'm saying, Paul Hamilton. You're mine. You've always been mine and always will be."

"Nurse?" He turned toward Jonica, who hastily prepared a hypodermic and stepped toward the ranting woman. "Lacy, we're going to give you something to make you sleep."

She turned her gaze from him to Jonica and screamed, "Get that cow out of here. Help, someone. She's trying to kill me! I saw her watching me." She aimed her rage at Jonica.

The special bustled back in through the open door. "What's going on in here?"

"That nurse is going to kill me," Lacy panted and strained away, eyes glazed with fear.

"Give her the hypodermic," Paul ordered.

An impulse she didn't understand caused Jonica to thrust the syringe into the special's hand. "You do it. I'm upsetting her."

The capable special seized the syringe, administered the dosage and ignored Lacy's shrieks that died as the medicine took effect. "Don't pay any attention to all her yelling," she said comfortingly. "Anesthesia does strange things to people." She shooed Jonica and Dr. Hamilton out. "Just leave her to me. Tomorrow she'll feel a lot differently."

Shaken, Jonica doubted it. When she finally got off duty and staggered to her room, she knew she'd never be able to sleep. Lacy's tantrum was especially out of place because of the loving aura that surrounded Shepherd of Love Hospital. The ugly taunts and unjust accusations hung in the air like a poison, marring the tranquillity that had come to mean so much even in the few short weeks Jonica had been there. She tossed and turned, snatching a little sleep but not enough.

A heavy feeling shrouded her spirit and when a knock came at her door in mid-afternoon, it didn't suprise her. She slipped into a robe and answered.

"Jonica, the Hospital Director has asked to see us." Dr. Hamilton stood in the hall, dark eyes brooding and sad.

"About last night?"

"I assume so. I'm sorry you have to be mixed up in all this." His honest face underscored just how much he regretted it. "Although it will probably turn out to be no more than a squall, it's never pleasant to have lies told about us." He sighed and cocked one eyebrow, then grinned. "Jesus told us to pray for those who despitefully use us.* Well, I guess He also meant those who *spitefully* accuse us, with no justification whatsoever." The grin faded, leaving his face bleak. "What I don't understand is why she has it in for you."

"I overheard your conversation, that time she talked with you in the Central Waiting Area when she said— you said. . ." She couldn't bring herself to repeat it.

"I see. Too bad I didn't see a long, long time ago. I suppose you've heard of my puppy love." His sense of humor evidently conquered his foreboding for he added, "Thank God He didn't allow it to become a dog's life." As if noticing for the first time she still wore a robe, he added, "I'll wait in the hall," and closed her door.

Jonica hastily donned a simple skirt and blouse, thrust her bare feet into sandals, brushed her teeth and hair and swiped a dash of lipstick on her trembling lips. She accompanied Dr. Hamilton to the Director's Office, matching her long free stride to his. Her heart sank at the look in the Hospital Director's eyes, the gravity in Nicholas Fairchild's, but the Director's opening words set her at ease.

"Before I tell you why I've called you here I want to reassure both of you—" he stressed the word *both*, "Nicholas and I have the fullest confidence in you."

Jonica wanted to thank him but couldn't. Fear such as she hadn't experienced since leaving high school

*Matthew 5:44 (KJV)

assailed her and her heart thudded to the soles of her feet when the kindly, troubled man went on.

"Mrs. Duncan has made some very serious charges against you. Ridiculous as they are, we have to face them. Jonica, she is charging you with an attempt to do her physical harm by giving her an injection."

"That is the most outrageous thing I've ever heard!" Paul Hamilton gritted his teeth. "What's she charging me with, aiding and abetting?"

"Far worse, Paul." Nicholas Fairchild looked older than Jonica had ever seen him. "She is threatening to sue you and the hospital for malpractice."

"For heaven's sake, why? I didn't even treat her!"

The Director's words fell like sharp stones on a smooth surface. "Not her. Mrs. Duncan accuses you of the wrongful death of her husband."

five

Jonica didn't realize she had bitten her lip until she tasted sweet-sickish blood. She blindly reached for a tissue in her pocket and pressed it to her mouth. Unbelievable. Was this all a nightmare that would end soon? If not, could it be a figment of her imagination? She removed the tissue. A small red stain brought her back to reality.

"It's bad enough accusing me—and I didn't even give her the injection," she fiercely stated. "But to charge Dr. Hamilton with such an obscene accusation is incredible! Every one of us in surgery knew it would take a miracle to save Mr. Duncan. Long after he was gone Dr. Hamilton and the others continued to work, trying every method to revive him." Angry tears threatened as she swallowed and regained her control. "Anyone who says anything different is a despicable liar."

Paul looked a bit taken aback at her warm defense, then the same odd look that had filled his eyes after surgery the night before crept into them. "Thank you, Jonica." He turned to the two men. "What do we do now? Shall I try and talk with her?"

"Absolutely not," the Director ordered. "That's evidently what she wants and she will construe it as a pacifying move."

"Can she actually get a lawyer who will represent her?" Jonica wondered aloud.

"Unfortunately, yes. There are always those notoriety-seeking attorneys who will take chances just for the publicity. However, we have one of the finest legal minds in the city available to us as well as the counsel of our Heavenly Father," Nicholas interjected. He smiled at Jonica.

"I wouldn't worry too much over this. It isn't the first and won't be the last time Shepherd of Love has faced persecution. We have always been guided and blessed."

The meeting ended with the promise they would get together again when the attorney could meet with them. Dr. Hamilton walked out with Jonica. "I wouldn't blame you if you picked up your belongings and fled, after this. Or at least, never wanted to see me again." He hesitated. "I was wondering, though. Would you consider going out to dinner with me tonight? It would get our minds off this mess."

"Why, I. . ."

"If it would make you feel more comfortable, we'll invite Emily and eat at my home," he told her. "She and Dad are old friends and I'd like for you to know my father." He eyed her. "Dad's a great cook."

"It sounds wonderful." Jonica silently ordered herself to settle down and read nothing more into the invitation than what was absolutely fact. Dr. Hamilton obviously felt sorry for her and hoped to soften Lacy's vindictiveness.

"I'll see that you and Emily get back in plenty of time for your shift," Paul promised and Jonica thought what a considerate person he was and such a good Christian. If more persons who believed and lived their faith as did Paul, probably a whole lot of people wouldn't be turned off by those who professed to be Christian. A little bell rang inside. Wasn't that what she did? She refused to let the bell clang. The prospect of a sort of date with her boss left no room for a psychological inquisition as to her motives.

Jonica's fatigue miraculously dwindled with a warm shower and the ritual of dressing. Her mint green summery dress, white sandals and purse were perfect. She snatched a lightweight sweater when Emily knocked. Seattle summer evenings cooled off.

"You certainly look nice," Emily told her.

"So do you. That soft pink shirtwaist style does things for your gray hair and eyes," Jonica responded honestly. The prospect of dinner with good friends brightened her face and raised her spirits. "Emily, you aren't trying to impress Mr. Hamilton, are you?"

Her right-hand nurse grunted but the pink in her cheeks deepened. "Would if I could," she said forthrightly. "Dr. Hamilton's a fine man. We're good friends, no more. I doubt that he will ever remarry. He had the best the first time around."

Jonica hugged the shorter woman. "I suppose you've been asked this a hundred times, but. . ." She broke off.

"You want to know why I haven't married." Emily's mischievous grin made her look like a pixie. "So do I." She ignored Jonica's peal of laughter and added, "I figured out that when I admired someone, he liked someone else. By the time several of them got around to noticing me, I had forgotten what it was I admired in them!" She laughed and her eyes twinkled. "Besides, I'd never marry anyone unless I believed with all my heart God wanted him in my life." She cast a shrewd glance at her tall supervisor. "I know He led me into nursing and to Shepherd of Love. If God ever wants me to marry, I'll know it. Not bad advice for some of you younger women, either."

"Not bad at all," Jonica soberly agreed, wondering why the thought that God might care enough about His followers' daily lives to actually help them choose a life's companion wisely should send such a surge of longing through her. Not for that companion, but for the relationship she sensed Emily shared with her Master.

Before she could examine the thought, Dr. Hamilton came loping down the hall toward them looking unnecessarily trim and attractive in well-creased slacks and a pale yellow shirt. "Ready, girls?" He made a face. "Uh, hope that doesn't offend you." Teasing anxiety lighted his dark eyes. "Today's women don't like to be called 'girls,' do they?"

"I do," Emily sturdily retorted. "Always will, too." An affectionate look softened her face into a broad smile. "At the risk of sounding over-eager, are you going to stand here all day or can we go eat?"

In the wave of laughter that followed Jonica escaped having to express her opinion on the girls-versus-women subject. Not that it mattered. She had a sneaking hunch it wouldn't matter what Dr. Paul Hamilton called her if he wore that relaxed, admiring smile that did tribute to the all-rightness of her ensemble.

The short drive from the hospital gave Jonica a chance to observe Paul. She'd insisted that Emily take the front passenger's seat and sat directly behind her. What a strong jaw and firm lips the doctor had. She liked the easy way his capable hands rested on the wheel, ready for whatever the other drivers might do. Once he swung sharply to miss a small cat who unwisely darted across the street.

Paul pulled into the driveway of his home and Jonica lingered outside for a moment after he courteously opened her door. "It's charming." Her curious gaze noted the sheltering maple filled with birds singing evening praise, the way the simple ranch style home clung to the ground amid shrubs and colorful flowers. Inside proved to be even more satisfying. The view of Mt. Rainier framed by white curtains in the dining room bay window awed her.

"You like our home." Peter Hamilton's observation jerked Jonica's fascinated gaze from the mountain.

"I love it." A gleam in the senior doctor's black eyes at their guest's fervent reply reflected in his son's across the room.

"We've kept it the way it was originally furnished," Paul said, as they sat down to their meal.

Dr. Peter offered prayer, then the conversation continued.

"You're smart," Emily asserted. She cut another bite of the delicious Swiss steak on her plate. "Too many people are going in for uncomfortable furniture just because it's stylish. Never could see why. If a person can't be comfortable in her own home, why have one?"

"So that's why you live in a staff suite," Paul teased.

Emily shrugged. "I might just surprise you and up and get married one of these days. Right, Jonica?"

Startled, Jonica snapped to attention from observing

the muted tones of rug and slip covers, the spotlessness that would do credit to an operating room and the feeling of peace that pervaded this home. "Sorry, I missed what you said." She laid down her fork and looked at Paul. "Now I know why you always look so calm. It's your home."

"It's mostly Dad and even more, our Heavenly Father."

She picked up her fork again and took a bite of crisp, icy salad. "You don't know how lucky you are." She sensed a rush of emotion and quickly changed the subject. "What kind of roses are they, Dr. Hamilton?" She sniffed the fragrance that vied with that of the excellent food and concentrated on the low centerpiece of cream roses with their rosy fuschia edges.

"Double Delight and they are." He smiled appreciatively. "But why not call me Peter, as Emily does? Or Dr. Peter, if you prefer?"

I wish I could have had a father like him, thought Jonica. The longing to know a true father's love almost overwhelmed her. She contrasted this godly man with her abusive stepfather and barely controlled a shudder. It's hard to believe both men were supposedly created in the image of God—the one who called on Him profanely; the other, whose face showed that he daily strove to become a reflection of their common Father.

The evening passed in a blur of laughter and warmth, one of the happiest Jonica had spent in years. She reluctantly told Dr. Peter good-bye when the time came for Paul to drive her and Emily back to the hospital. "I can't tell you how much it's meant," she said in a low voice.

"Come back any time, my dear." Dr. Peter's keen black eyes smiled as well as his mobile mouth. He pressed her hand. "I'm here most of the time, at least for a while longer. Don't wait for a formal invitation. I really mean that."

She knew he did. She also had a feeling that if she were ever in real trouble, her new friend would back her to whatever limits necessary.

On the short ride to Shepherd of Love, Jonica suddenly realized something. "Why, we didn't talk about Mrs. Jones-Duncan at all."

"On purpose." Paul's eyes, so like his father's, filled with mischief. She could see them in the corner of the rearview mirror. "Dad and I have a standing rule not to ruin good food with problems we can't solve. Time enough later to discuss them." He shrugged his wide shoulders. "God will have to take care of it, probably using our hospital attorney on call."

"I dread going back on duty tonight," Jonica whispered.

"Don't. Lacy asked for and received a transfer to a private center that caters to the elite, although she could just as well have gone home and returned to Outpatient for change of dressings."

"Good thing she didn't." Emily bounced a little in spite of her seat belt. "Patty Thompson works there and she is not a fan of Lacy Jones-Duncan in the least."

Jonica hid a grin, remembering Patty's mother hen act and her identifying the troublemaker as Her Nibs and the Queen of Sheba. Just knowing she wouldn't have to contend with Lacy made going on duty a pleasure.

One of the things the night charge nurse liked best about Shepherd of Love Hospital was the lack of kowtowing to the rich or treating nonpaying patients as unworthy. Each patient received the same quality care, compassion and interest. Shortly after Jonica arrived, she overheard a new nurse speak angrily to a patient. Three days later the nurse was dismissed. "She lost the whole point of our service," Nancy Galbraith said at the supper table that night. At the other end of the spectrum, the former recluse who had given land for the hospital ended up in a ward when he came over from the Retirement Center for observation. Semiprivate rooms were filled and the hospital didn't move one patient to make room for another except in critical cases.

The generous donor's comment, "Treats 'em all alike," plus his added, "Good," swept through the hospital grapevine.

ра

A few dark clouds loomed on the fair skies of Jonica's new world. Lacy Jones-Duncan persisted in her hate suit, although rumor had it a dozen lawyers turned her down before she hired a tacky attorney who advertised on TV and billboards. He agreed to take her case on a 40 percent contingency basis—a hefty chunk if she won her $5,000,000 civil suit. He immediately filed the complaint against Dr. Paul Hamilton and Shepherd of Love Hospital.

"Why the hospital?" Jonica wondered.

"She knows Paul doesn't have the money," their attorney explained. "In legal terms, the hospital is the 'deep pocket,' or the source of funds."

"What happens now?"

"Her counsel has walked the complaint into court and we've received copies; a court date will be put on the docket." He smiled. "It doesn't mean a thing. They need a prima facie case to win—that means self-evident, valid—which they don't have. You'll also note no mention is made of the earlier accusations toward Miss Carr. A fisherman like this one doesn't bother with sardines when he's out for whales."

"Thank God for that," Paul put in.

Their keen-eyed lawyer continued, "My office will begin the discovery process which is to gather medical records including the autopsy and depositions, statements from witnesses, and so on. We then prepare and file a motion for summary judgement that shows Mrs. Jones-Duncan's claim is without merit. Copies go to her attorney. Time is allowed for a response and claims or counterclaims, if any. The judge will call in counsel for both parties and, unless I'm grossly mistaken, will rule that the allegations are totally unfounded and end the whole thing." His eyes twinkled.

"Then I won't even have to appear?" Paul asked.

"Not unless the judge denies my motion for summary judgment and he won't." Confidence underscored every word of the prediction.

A few weeks later Jonica and Paul were again summoned to the lawyer's office. "Good news," he announced. "The judge really let the plaintiff's attorney have it." He leaned back in his chair and laughed broadly. "Told him the case was ludicrous, then went a step farther and fined the attorney. He will be required to pay all defense attorney's fees."

"What?" Jonica stared. "How could he do that?"

"There's a rule which states lawyers may not file cases that have no justification. It's designed to prevent unscrupulous lawyers from clogging the courts with such cases." He rose, shook hands with each of them and advised, "I'd forget the whole thing if I were you."

The letdown left Jonica feeling a bit shaky. When they went outside, Paul smiled at her. "All right?"

"I think so. I'm just glad it's all over. How could you be so calm all through this?"

"Dad and I prepared with prayer."

Tapping heels on the sidewalk announced Lacy Jones-Duncan's arrival. "Oh, Paul," she cried. "That awful lawyer insisted I sue you."

"Strange that an attorney hires a client. If you'll excuse us, we have things to do," Paul disdainfully told her.

Lacy turned toward Jonica. "This is all your fault," she furiously accused the nurse who had unwillingly witnessed her double humiliation. "Don't think he will ever fall for you."

Her brittle laugh could have shattered fine crystal.

"Remember this. I keep what's mine even if I no longer want it and Paul Hamilton has been my property since the day I turned sixteen." She turned and ran down the sidewalk.

"Too bad to waste such a dramatic exit on such a small audience," Paul observed, although Jonica noticed how a little twitch in his cheek showed anger. "She's wrong, you known. My only interest in her is the concern I have for anyone who flouts God and His laws." His eyes glowed and he suddenly laughed. "She's also wrong about something else. I not only could be

interested in someone like you, I am. Very interested."
With a squeeze of her hand that sent stars shooting into
her brain, he smiled and turned away when the hospital
attorney called him.

Jonica floated through the next weeks. Never had an
autumn been more beautiful. Maple yellow and sumac
red painted the hills around Seattle. Late roses nodded,
bloomed and nodded again. Dahlias and goldenrod
added their color and crispy nights cooled the city but
no frost came. A time of transition, she thought one
afternoon when she and Lindsey finished a strenuous
workout on the hospital tennis courts. A period of quiet
in between the past and the future, one to be enjoyed
for itself. On days like this, filled with activity and the
challenge of her night work, Jonica felt herself unwind-
ing. Lindsey and her other nurse friends who clustered
at one end of the staff quarters provided diversion, while
Paul—she didn't finish her musing.

"Did you hear the latest?" Lindsey flung her racket
on the grass and herself into a lawn chaise.

Jonica followed suit. "What latest?"

"Our late but not missed patient Ms. Lacy Jones-
Duncan is back."

"Back? I didn't know she'd gone away."

"Oh, my, yes." Lindsey rolled her eyes. "Didn't you
see the big news splash that 'the grieving widow of one
of our illustrious citizens, whose untimely death left
her prostrated, observed a period of mourning aboard a
private yacht, but has bravely returned to her lovely
Seattle home that holds so many precious memories.'
A lot of hooey, if you ask me." She brushed away a
drop of perspiration from her freckled nose and cocked

a reddish eyebrow. "Hope she doesn't try to get her painted claws into Doc Hamilton." A wide grin spread and she stretched. "I actually don't think it's possible, what with him spending every spare minute escorting a certain night charge nurse about."

Jonica glanced down but couldn't help the smile that curved her lips. "That has to be his decision."

"Oh?"

Jonica mimicked her friend to perfection. "I don't see any signs of warfare concerning the young doctor who hangs over your shoulder whenever he can."

"Hey, that's different." Lindsey sat up straight and smoothed her rumpled red curly hair before admitting, "I guess I'm just talking. If I have to snare a guy, I don't want him."

She leaned forward and her mischief died. "Jonica, Dr. Paul's a great man and a wonderful Christian. I think he's learning to care for you and I don't blame him a bit. The rest of us hero worship him but you're different, more mature. You have our collective blessing. You're a grand person." She cleared her voice of huskiness and seriousness at the same time and the brown eyes glinted gold. "Not a bad boss, either."

The two headed for showers arm in arm and laughing, but a little gray cloud persisted. Could she ever be good enough for Paul?

Shina Ito had moved into the pretty yellow suite shortly after Jonica arrived. She had also invited her special friends home with her for authentic Japanese cuisine. The nurses enjoyed the food and cordial welcome, although as Patty said afterwards, "I can see why it took you so long to convince your parents you should live at Shepherd of Love."

Shina smiled. "My parents are very traditional except they are Christian. I am so glad." Her move gave Jonica time to know the small nurse better and she liked what she saw.

"Funny how you and I, Patty and Lindsey, Shina and Emily kind of hang together," she told Nancy Galbraith one day when she followed up a surgical case to Pediatrics, where her little patient recuperated.

"We all live at the one end of the hall," Nancy told her practically. "The nurses at the other end do the same, except more of them come and go while we're permanent."

For the second time Jonica found questions trembling on her lips. Nancy never referred to her past, never mentioned plans for the future. Friendly and extremely efficient, she joined in with the younger nurses yet didn't chatter or share as they did. Jonica respected her privacy, yet couldn't help wondering why such a beautiful person wasn't sought after. Once she noticed a soft look in the shining dark eyes and face when Dr. Damon Barton, an on-call children's specialist from private practice, came in for a consultation. Tall and well built, Dr. Barton's warm dark skin and flashing eyes commanded attention. Nancy's expression changed immediately—yet Jonica still wondered.

six

"Jonica Carr is the most restful woman I have ever known." Paul Hamilton's remark fell into the companionable silence he and his father often shared, especially when the autumn evenings grew chill and they set the small gas fireplace glowing.

"She has changed immeasurably since the first time she came here," Peter commented. "I sensed tension in her and conflict; not all because of Lacy Duncan's persecution, either. Now, there is peace. I believe God is working in her life."

Doubt crept into the younger doctor's voice. "She said she was a Christian on her application."

"Not all Christians have the peace of God in their souls," his father sighed. "I don't mean to pry, but do you care for Jonica?"

"I admire and respect her. I like the way she stands up to life. I appreciate her strength, even when I catch sight of a lost little girl lurking in her eyes at times." Paul stared into the flames. "At those times I long to put my arms around her and offer my protection for always. Yes, Dad, I care for her."

"Have you told her?"

"Not in words. I have a feeling she can't be rushed." He suddenly laughed. "To think I ever considered marrying Lacy when a woman such as Jonica exists. It hardly seems possible."

"She reminds me of your mother in some ways." Shadows hid Peter's face.

"You still miss her, after all these years." Not a question, but a statement.

"Yes. I always will."

The simple words brought mist to Paul's eyes. "Dad, have you ever considered remarrying?"

"Yes. How would you feel about it?"

Paul had the feeling a great deal rested on his response. He considered for a long moment before saying, "Until I met Jonica I think I would have resented it."

"And now?"

Again that sense of urgency came. "Someday I'll marry and establish a home of my own. I hate to think of you being alone. I think Mother would feel the same."

Peter stretched his hand out to his son, who clasped it in a hard shake. "There's something I need to share with you. No woman can ever fill your mother's place. Yet in the past months I've looked ahead. Paul, do you know one of the saddest things about being alone, especially after the death of a beloved companion? It isn't what most people think—the loss of intimacy; it's knowing you don't have someone to grow old with. God willing, I can look forward to many years ahead, busy years now that I'm physically better. As you say, one day you will be gone. That's as it should be. Lately I've felt the need to make room in my heart not for a replacement love, but for an additional love; new feelings, shared interest, but I. . ."

"Didn't know how I'd feel." Paul supplied the missing words. The phrase "knowing you don't have someone to grow old with" had struck deep. "Dad, is it

Emily Davis?"

"It might be." The dark eyes flashed. "If she'll have an old codger like me. Our friendship goes back to the time of your mother. Of course, the real test is whether we both feel God is directing us."

"I know what you mean. I'm still working on that about Jonica," his son said. "Dad, thanks." He didn't add, thanks for sharing your holy of holies with me. Dad would know. He always did.

æ

By Thanksgiving Paul knew he loved Jonica with the deep devotion of marriage. He suspected his father knew it as well. Peter confirmed it by asking, "What are you waiting for?" outright on Thanksgiving evening when Emily and Jonica had gone after sharing the Hamiltons' day.

"There's something I have to settle in my own mind first." Why hadn't he told Dad weeks before, Paul chastised himself.

His mouth dropped open when Peter quietly said, "You're going to leave Shepherd of Love."

"How did you know?"

His father's dark eyes flashed. "A good father knows a lot about his son. That's why God knew Jesus would carry out His mission on earth." He paused. "Where is it you are being called?"

"To a new ministry." Spoken aloud, the feelings he had dealt with for months took on reality. "Dad, I've given all I have to medicine. I've loved it, but it isn't enough. Six months or so ago I happened to drive through a downtown area I hadn't seen for ages. Hurting people, some vacant-faced, others empty-eyed, lined the streets. Girls barely into their teens turned tricks. Men, women and children slept in doorways because the overflowing shelters ran out of space.

"Such things ought not to be!" Paul fired to the subject, stood and paced the room. "These are children of God, too, or could be if more persons cared. The various organizations such as the Union Gospel Mission and Salvation Army perform miracles, yet they can't do everything."

"What is God asking you to do?"

Paul had the curious feeling his entire life had pointed to this moment. "I believe I am to set up a combination clinic, with Shepherd of Love standards that allow treatment for all whether or not they can pay. A clinic that requires Christian personnel and offers shelter to the needy until a place can be found for them elsewhere." He took a deep breath and added, "I also believe I must study in my off-hours until I can be a lay preacher as well as a doctor. I need to know scripture backward and forward so when the medical skills fail, God can use me as a bedside pastor."

Peter didn't speak for a long time. When he did, Paul heard excitement and hesitancy in his father's voice. "And Jonica?"

Some of his enthusiasm trickled away. "If she truly loves me, she will follow. If not—" He spread his hands. "I have to take orders from my Chief."

A quick intake of breath betrayed the older doctor's emotion.

"Son, for the past several weeks I've known I'm ready to go back to work but have held off. I haven't known why, yet have rather dreaded it." His face shone. "Can you use some help at your clinic and shelter? I wouldn't mind selling my practice and changing to a new and exciting ministry." He drummed his fingers on the arm of his chair. "I think we need to go see Nicholas Fairchild. He had a dream given by God and carried it out. He can give us a lot of good advice."

Seventy-one-year-old Nicholas looked younger than he had at sixty-five when father and son presented their dream to him. His blue eyes glistened with renewed vigor. "Now that the hospital is doing well, paying its own way, why, I'd like to invest in your plan," he enthused. "Why not make it an offshoot and call it Shepherd of Love Sanctuary? That implies rescue and help, the things Jesus taught in His ministry."

Paul felt so overwhelmed after the initial meeting with Nicholas that he told his father on the way home, "I can't believe how smoothly it went. It's as if God had prepared him to receive the idea before we ever walked into his house."

"Who's to say He didn't?" Peter chuckled. "Remember how Nicholas sprang the original hospital idea on a skeptical Seattle, only to discover God had gone ahead of him in every aspect. Paul, when people discover God's will and prepare to do it, He unties knots we don't even know exist. One thing, though." He cleared his throat. "You and I had best be talking things over with Jonica and Emily or if I know Nicholas Fairchild—and I do—the Shepherd of Love Sanctuary will be built and in operation before we can say thanks!"

৯

Jonica turned from her phone, well pleased. "Wonder why Paul sounded so excited?" she murmured. Her heart leaped. When had she known Dr. Hamilton was the man she had dreamed of for years? The first night she came to the hospital? The first time he performed surgery and she assisted? In the stuffy hospital room where Lacy Jones-Duncan maintained he belonged to her? Or had she come to love him gradually, the way a rosebud slowly opens to light and rain and sunshine, unfolding in beauty and fragrance.

A light knock at the door summoned her. Emily Davis stood there. "I just received the strangest call from Peter Hamilton," she said and came inside. "I've never heard him sound so—so officious. He almost ordered me to be ready to be picked up in thirty minutes." She dropped into a chair, indignation spoiled by a rather pleased smile.

"That's odd. I got the same kind of call from Paul," Jonica told her. "What could be up? You've been seeing a lot of Dr. Peter, haven't you?"

"Yes and I intend to go on doing the same," the peppery nurse stated. "Jonica, I believe he is going to ask me to marry him and don't think I'll hesitate before saying yes."

"You said once you'd have to know God wanted you to marry."

"I do." Happiness filled Emily's countenance and an assurance the younger nurse envied. "This is one of the finest gifts God has given me. Peter will never love me as he did Paul's mother. I know that and don't care. He will love me in a different manner, one all my own and special. There are many kinds of love and ours will be blessed by God." Her kind eyes looked straight into Jonica's. "So will yours and Paul's, if you accept him."

"He's never said he loved me." Jonica turned her back, unwilling to hope for something when she felt so unworthy.

"Wrong. He has silently shouted it in a dozen ways," Emily contradicted. "Don't be surprised if I become your, uh, would it be stepmother-in-law?"

"You're incorrigible!" Jonica whipped around and giggled.

"I know, but I'm nice. Smug, too." Emily ducked out the door, slammed it behind her and left Jonica to get ready for Paul.

When Paul arrived, the look in his eyes set Jonica's heart racing the way it had a few weeks earlier when he kissed her for the first time. Yet more than physical attraction, the sense of having come home filled her—the feeling nothing on earth would ever hurt her again as long as Dr. Hamilton stayed near. Now the wild-rose slacks and jacket outfit she wore paled by comparison with her burning face. She tried to hide it by casually remarking, "Emily said your father called her."

"Yes." Paul laughed in sheer exuberance. "We're going our separate ways, however." He ushered her out, put her into his car as if she were something inestimably precious, then climbed behind the wheel and started the motor.

Heavy traffic required his attention and Jonica sat beside him, content just to be with him. He reached I-5, headed south and cut off on I-405, working his way south and east. A succession of smaller roads brought them to a forested area that overlooked Mt. Rainier, a peaceful valley and a shining river. Paul pulled into a roadside area.

"Come, Jonica."

He bounded out of the car, opened her door and took her hand. A short climb led to a bench placed to make the most of the view. Paul put his arm around her shoulders and for a long moment they watched afternoon shadows gather.

She shivered, more with excitement than from the cold, although the late November sun's rays held little warmth.

Again Paul said, "Come." He led her back to the car. Once inside he quietly told her, "Jonica, I love you. I always will. If you will marry me, we can make life all it should be, serving together and honoring our God."

Roman candles of joy shot through her. She opened her mouth to speak but Paul lightly placed a hand over her lips.

"Before you say anything, I must tell you some news. First, do you love me?"

She could only nod speechlessly.

"Then perhaps it will be all right." He took his hand away and smiled. "I still want to explain before you make promises you might regret."

Her heart beat painfully. It couldn't be that this fine man meant to confess an unholy past, something to do with Lacy Jones-Duncan, could it? Where had that poisonous thought come from? She would stake her life on Paul's honor.

"It wouldn't be fair to ask you to marry me when I'm Chief Surgeon at Shepherd of Love, then spring my news on you," Paul said. His dark eyes looked troubled, not shining and happy as they had a few moments earlier. "I'm leaving the hospital."

An involuntary gasp escaped her lips. She stared at him. What on earth. . .? Her world rocked.

"For months, even before you came, restlessness inside me and a feeling of urgency has let me know God wanted something more than I've been doing." Paul spread his hands wide. An excited gleam replaced some of the shadow in his dark eyes. "I told Dad and he confirmed the rightness of my decision—he's been ready to get back to practicing medicine but holding off for the same reason: the feeling his practice isn't where he needs to be." Paul looked like a boy with a new kite, all enthusiasm and expectations.

Jonica longed to assure him it didn't matter where he went, she'd trail along. She couldn't get the words out. What kind of man was this, who calmly walked away from a prestigious position where he was loved and respected because he felt God wanted him to do another job? *I really don't know him at all*, she thought, fingers tightly clutched. *I knew he trusted his Master, but this is incredible. I'll never understand his trust and obedience to God, but how I wish I could.*

She finally found her voice. "Where are you going?" It came out as a whisper, sounding strained and fearful.

Paul glanced out the window, back in the direction they had come. "To the highways and byways."

All the insecurity Jonica had fought for years rushed over her. They increased when Paul continued.

"Dad and I, under Nicholas Fairchild's sponsorship, are going to establish a Shepherd of Love Sanctuary in the hard-core area of Seattle to bring healing and salvation to those who need it most."

She shrank back from him until her shoulders pushed

hard against the car door. "No, oh, no!" She blindly held her hands out, pushing away the poverty, misery and abuse she had run away from ten years earlier. A feeling of revulsion washed through her.

"Jonica, what is it?" Face colorless, Paul took her cold, shaking hands in his warm ones. The concern in his voice proved too much. Tearing sobs shattered the peacefulness in the car.

"I can't go back. I can't. Oh, Paul don't make me go back!"

A river of hot tears pressed behind her eyelids. If they once fell, she could never stop crying. Jonica freed her hands and groped in her purse for a tissue, pressing it against her burning eyes.

Paul sat stone-still, asking no questions. Through her own agony, she could see his suffering and tried to explain. "I came from such an area. I vowed I'd never go back. My stepfather. . ." She shuddered.

"Did he hurt you?" Steel laced his voice.

"Only by making our home miserable and wearing my mother down with his drinking and cursing. I can't remember a time they weren't fighting over something, usually money."

"You wouldn't have to work at the Sanctuary," Paul said in an even voice that held not the slightest hint of condemnation.

Jonica could sense his bitter disappointment. He had come to her with bright hopes of their working side by side under the command of God. She had destroyed his dreams, able only to offer a half loaf. Paul needed a wife who would share and support him, not one who hated his work and resented it. Even if she kept on at

Shepherd of Love and they lived far from the new ministry, its shadow couldn't help reaching out toward them and eventually swallowing her up. Why, God? her heart desperately asked, knowing Paul had irrevocably set his face in the way he believed he must go. With or without her, Dr. Paul Hamilton would follow wherever his Master led. If his heart ached for a woman who would not, no, could not join him, his patients would never suspect.

And what of her? Now that her long-held dream had come so close to being realized, then snatched from her by some capricious quirk, must she slink away to lick her wounds, hoping to heal but knowing herself prey to bitterness beyond anything she had ever known? The prospect appalled her. "Paul." Her voice shook. "Are you certain?"

He stared at her. Compassion filled his eyes but his face went haggard. "Yes, Jonica, I am. I know this is a shock. Couldn't you think about it?" A note of hope persisted through his despair.

Eager to postpone a jagged break that would leave her bleeding inside, she assented. "Yes." She snatched the reprieve as a condemned prisoner grabs a pardon. Would even sharing Paul with down-and-outers be worse than losing his love forever? Her confused heart and mind clung to the question, for which she had no answer—yet.

Paul didn't push it. Instead, he tenderly kissed her lips and started the motor. If Jonica lived to be a hundred, she would never forget the love, resignation and sadness in his face during the long drive home. When he left her at her door, he kissed her again and told her,

"I'll be praying for you."

Even through her abstraction, she noticed he hadn't said for us. Had he subconsciously accepted her protest as final? She stood in a warm shower for what felt like ages, willing the water to scrub away her doubts and uncertainties. Why couldn't she be like that Biblical woman—Ruth, wasn't it? The one who said whither thou goest. The thought haunted her and when she dried and slipped into a warm gown, she crawled into bed and opened her Bible. Thank God she had the night off. Her lip curled. Why should she thank God for such a trivial thing when He had just taken Paul from her? She remembered a sermon in which the pastor had said God was a jealous God. Perhaps He didn't want Paul getting entangled with a person like her who had never really come to know Him.

She sighed, found the Book of Ruth and read the age-old love story. The oft-quoted words of the heart of it shimmered behind a fine mist.

> *Intreat me not to leave thee, or to return from*
> *following after thee: for whither thou goest,*
> *I will go; and where thou lodgest, I will lodge:*
> *thy people shall be my people, and thy God*
> *my God.**

The Bible slid from her weak fingers to the coverlet. Jonica closed her eyes against the beauty of the promise and the pain that assailed her. Ruth had given her vow to a mother- in-law. Why, then, couldn't a modern Ruth do the same for the man she loved with all the pent-up feelings of years that longed to pour themselves out?

*Ruth 1:16 (KJV)

She tried to pray. "Lord, if it were anywhere except . . ." The words died on her lips. She thought of Ruth again, her love for her mother-in-law. It paled in comparison with the love Jonica felt for Peter Hamilton. She had come to look on him as the father she always wanted and she knew he returned her love. How would he react when he learned she had rejected his son because she would not follow him to the Sanctuary?

A picture of him came to mind. His steady eyes held regret but not an ounce of condemnation, just as his son's eyes had done earlier.

"God, why can't You be as loving and understanding as Peter is?" she cried. "He would never let his son's heart break by sending him into a place that won't even want him." Fear gripped her. She knew such areas; Paul did not. "God, some will hate him. They may even try to kill him."

The deepest flash of insight she had ever experienced planted words in her heart and mind. God had sent His Son to a place that didn't want Him. Some hated Him. Those who chose wickedness killed Him, the very ones He came to save.

All night Jonica struggled, alternating between an honest desire to know God for her own sake as well as Paul's and the feeling her prayers never got beyond the ceiling of her room.

seven

By morning, Jonica had gone from shock and disbelief to numbness and apathetic acceptance. Although it meant renouncing every promise she had made to herself, she had no choice. Nothing—even going back—could be worse than losing Paul. Yet little joy came with her decision. She dreaded seeing him and wondered if she were actress enough to convince him how much she'd changed overnight.

Unfortunately for her good intentions, Paul didn't appear. A brief note lay on her floor, evidently slipped beneath her door while she uneasily slept.

> *Darling,*
> *Dad and I are going out of town for a few*
> *days. I regret it, particularly at this time.*
> *On the other hand, you'll have some time*
> *to think.*
>
> *I love you.*
> *Paul.*

"I'd be better off with time not to think," she said. She stuck the note under her pillow, comforted but more torn than ever. Paul deserved more than deceit and hiding her real feelings. Was it right to marry him and embark on a lifetime of keeping back resentment? In time, he would surely detect it. What then? She stubbornly set her mouth. It hadn't been right for God to let her meet Paul, then call him to chase off to the very place she had despised and escaped from.

Up and down, back and forth, her thoughts swung. At times she felt she must flee, simply disappear at least until she could sort things out. Yet the upcoming holiday season meant increased accidents and she'd be needed. How could she turn her back on those who desperately depended on good care?

Neither can Paul turn his back on those who need him, a little voice reminded. She ignored it and channeled her energy into working harder than ever. If her friends noticed she had grown quieter, they had little time to consider why. Christmas at Shepherd of Love meant added carol practices, decorating and the cooperation of the staff so those who could not be home might still have a happy day.

Letters from Paul told that he and Peter had been detained in Portland. Contacts with persons who might be instrumental in helping establish the Sanctuary meant long hours. Yet, Paul wrote, more and more he realized the validity of the plan. God had obviously gone ahead of them and prepared hearts. There was talk that once the Seattle Sanctuary got going, concerned Christians with financial and spiritual resources wanted another built in Portland.

The news disturbed Jonica even more. In Paul's absence she had begun to feel it might not be so bad. As he said, she need not be personally involved. She could continue working in her cherished position until children arrived. Now it became clear that the Seattle Sanctuary would only be a beginning. A long procession of years in which Paul gave the majority of his time and life to the needy gnawed at the woman who loved him. Where did she fit in?

"I could handle being second, when God is first," she told herself. "But once Paul gets into this, where will I be on his totem pole of importance—third, or down below those who come for help?" The corroding bitterness she feared continually hounded her with such thoughts until she dreaded contact with Emily.

The gray-eyed, gray-haired woman's sturdy shoes still clung to the ground but her heart floated. "To think I'll not only be Peter's wife but be able to work with him where we are most needed," she'd exclaimed the day after the fateful evening when she became engaged and Jonica did not. "Aren't you excited?"

"Ummm." Jonica didn't commit herself and Emily subsided. The younger nurse suspected her friend's keen eyes had seen something was amiss but Emily never pried. She and Peter planned to be quietly married in the Hospital Chapel with only a few close friends present and a short honeymoon to the San Juan Islands. The new Mrs. Hamilton would continue in her job until the Sanctuary had been built.

Jonica thought she had made up her mind to tell Paul she couldn't marry him by the time he returned. Yet one evening when he strode into surgery, gowned, masked and ready to operate as a special favor to the Hospital Director, her heart turned traitor. Outwardly steady, they worked as two blades on a pair of fine scissors. The poignant light in his eyes didn't detract one iota from the skill that saved the life of their patient, an elderly man with internal bleeding.

They finished their task, cleaned up and Jonica knew no matter what the cost, she could never send him away.

"I'll be waiting when you get off," he told her quietly.

"I'm glad." She watched him go out, sighed and turned back to her duties. A niggling little sense of emptiness accompanied her on her rounds. Like Ruth, she would follow. Unlike Ruth, it must be with reservations.

"The Chapel will be empty at this hour," Paul told her when she stepped into the hall after giving her morning report to the next shift's charge nurse. He smiled down at her and she wondered, why does it all seem so right and easy when he's with me, so impossible when we're apart?

The Chapel shone with fresh wax, soft light and red roses. They walked to the front and stood beneath a fine lithograph of Sallman's Head of Christ. "Well, Jonica?"

She looked up at him, knowing her heart shone through her yes. "'Whither thou goest, Paul.'" She hastily averted her gaze from the humility she saw in his lean face. Something cold slipped onto her ring finger. She looked down. A plain gold band with the purest of diamonds glittered on her finger. It felt heavy and she suppressed a quiver, realizing the weight came not from the solitaire but from all it represented. The desire to be honest caused her to say, "I still have doubts."

"Not about our love." He looked shocked.

"No." Of that she could be sure.

"Then it will be all right, my darling." He drew her

close, held her head next to his heart and stroked her hair. The positive note in his voice stilled beating wings of uncertainty and Jonica relaxed in his arms, silently pledging herself to become worthy of his love.

Jonica refused to formally announce their engagement until after Peter and Emily's wedding She told Paul, "Let's keep our secret. I'll wear my ring on a chain under my uniform. I can't wear it during surgery, anyway."

"I'm ready to shout it from the hospital roof." Paul cocked a dark eyebrow at her. "I doubt that we'll have to announce it as far as Dad is concerned. He's pretty shrewd and commented he liked hearing me sing around the house for the past few weeks. Guess my feelings are like a barometer."

"My special nurse friends are just as bad. I catch sly knowing looks," Jonica sighed. She couldn't put into words how precious it felt to hug their engagement close to her for a time. Once it became public knowledge, a little of the special privacy she shared with Paul alone would be lost in congratulations and plans.

"How about announcing it on New Year's Eve—Dad and Emily will be back then—and we can get married as soon as we can get a license?" Paul suggested.

She hesitated, struggling with her feelings. "Would you think I'm too sentimental if I told you I'd like to be married on Valentine's Day?"

Paul's dark eyes smiled even before his lips curled into the heart-melting expression she loved. "I'd think you were just what I want, for always. Someone who isn't afraid to show honest sentiment and ask for what she wants." His laugh rang out. "Exactly what the doctor ordered."

The strength of his caring wove a protective web around Jonica and helped her laugh at her fears. Surely they could find happiness when their deep love combined with dedicated service to others. She resolutely put aside an inner awareness of the chasm between them concerning deep faith.

She still couldn't trust God for all things. Paul did. In an effort to be more like him, she spent time studying the scriptures and ended up more confused than ever. Her heart leaped when she read First Corinthians 7:14:

> *For the unbelieving husband is sanctified by the wife, and the unbelieving wife is sanctified by the husband.* *

Didn't that more than cover her situation? She certainly wasn't an unbeliever; she just didn't know God the way Paul did.

Yet verses that talked about being unequally yoked and building a house on sand chilled her. Most of the time she could overcome them and be happy, yet now and then, especially if she were overtired, she took them out and faced the fact that she needed to tell Paul exactly how she felt. Each time, she refused. How could anyone so strong understand the scars from childhood that left her weak and unable to give wholehearted devotion to a God she couldn't see?

❧

Emily became Mrs. Hamilton. Jonica wept at the candlelit service that was more a sacrament than a ceremony. Twin flames in Paul's eyes glowed in her heart,

*KJV

as did his low, "We're next."

Christmas passed with a minimum of patients and lots of special activities for those unable to go home. January found Paul deep in plans for Shepherd of Love Sanctuary. He had been asked to speak at several churches, not to raise money but to let people know why the combination clinic and shelter was being built. He closed with almost the identical statement Nicholas Fairchild had used years before—that no pleas for finances would be made. If some hearers felt God wanted them to be part of it, gifts would be gladly accepted but no public credit given to any givers.

To both his and Jonica's amazement, Lacy Jones-Duncan sought them out after the service. She hadn't been around since her inglorious legal defeat. Every blond curl sparkled. So did her blue eyes. Toned-down makeup gave her a softer look. Instead of gushing, she said with a hint of wistfulness, Jonica couldn't decide whether real or fake, "I'd love to be part of your new venture." She glanced down so her lashes covered her eyes, then looked up appealingly. "I saw the announcement of your engagement in the paper, Paul. I'm terribly sorry I ever accused you. Forgive me, and let me help. My—husband left me a lot of money."

"You heard the condition," Paul reminded. A little frown drew his brows together.

"Thank you. You'll be hearing from me." She gave him a dazzling smile, then turned to Jonica. Safe from Paul's gaze, the smile froze. "Congratulations, nurse. You have a fine man." She moved away to let others speak to them.

"Wonder what she's up to?" Paul looked after the

trim figure. "She sounded sorry but I still can't help being suspicious."

So did Jonica, although she wisely kept it to herself. But when Lacy presented Paul with a six-figure check and continued to enthusiastically spread the word about the new Sanctuary, it appeared she had really changed. She made a point of seeking out Jonica, prattling of hospital and clinic matters, though the beleaguered nurse wondered how she learned so much. In spite of Lacy's repeated protestations of repentance, Jonica didn't trust her and had a hard time not showing it. Lacy also became a thistle in the newly-engaged nurse's little garden of Eden with her laughing reminder about the "childhood romance," as she called it, she and Paul had shared.

"Why, at one time, neither of us ever thought there could be anyone else," she confided once.

Stung, Jonica shot back, "Obviously there was and is."

Lacy laughed. "I'm sorry I offended you. I still consider Paul and his father among my dearest friends and I wouldn't want anything to ever come between us."

Jonica nobly bit her tongue and resisted the temptation to walk away and leave the "dear friend" standing there with her mouth open.

A two-day storm arrived the end of January. The snow all but paralyzed the city. Shepherd of Love had its own backup system and suffered less than many but stranded doctors and nurses doubled up with residents of the staff who lived at the hospital complex. Nancy Galbraith moved in with Jonica for overnight and insisted she would be perfectly comfortable on the couch. Patty and Lindsey made room for Shina and freed up another room. Off duty, Jonica enjoyed an evening with a large group of interns and nurses in the big living room, swapping stories and eating popcorn. But the time she shared with Nancy meant the most.

"I don't want to pry, but is everything all right with you and Paul?" Nancy hesitantly asked.

"Practically perfect."

"Just practically?" The warm brown eyes held reservations.

"You know how it is. We're both so busy we don't see as much of each other as I'd like and—"

"And Ms. Jones-Duncan hovers when you could." Nancy shook her head. "I may be unChristian but sometimes I wonder how much the leopard really changes its spots."

"I do, too. Yet she acts so friendly I alternate between feeling guilty about my doubts and still having them."

Nancy stretched and yawned. "I wouldn't trust her a full hundred percent and I hope you won't either." She yawned again. "On the other hand, I'm something of an alarmist at times." A smile showed beautiful white teeth. "Sorry, Jonica. I'm not bored, just dead on my feet. Mind if I turn in?"

"Not at all." Yet when her friend lay sleeping Jonica mulled over Nancy's comments. In the months at Shepherd of Love she had seldom heard the other nurse criticize anyone. The fact she evidently thought it necessary set off a warning signal in Jonica's mind. However, day followed day until Valentine's Day lay just a week ahead.

Exhausted by an unusually heavy schedule, all Jonica

wanted was to peel off her uniform, soak in a tub and sleep the clock around. She had the next two weeks off with plenty of time for wedding preparations and the short honeymoon that would nearly duplicate Peter and Emily's. She followed her program as far as the bath and wrapped herself in a fluffy aqua robe. She'd give herself a few minutes to unwind before going to bed. Once there, she had a feeling it would take Gabriel's horn to awaken her.

A staccato knock brought a groan. What now? Residents of staff quarters religiously observed the DO NOT DISTURB signs when posted on doors and Jonica had put hers out.

The knock came again and a petulant voice calling, "Jonica, answer the door. It's Lacy."

Muttering something more disgusted than elegant, the tired charge nurse reluctantly let her unwelcome visitor in but said, "I'm really tired. Could you come another time?"

"This won't take long and it can't wait." Lacy swished in on a wave of perfume, fairly radiating excitement. "All this time I've held back but no longer. You can't marry Paul. He's mine, as I told you months ago." She closed the door behind her.

Indignation wiped out Jonica's fatigue. "I suggest you go." She started toward the door.

"Not until you read this." Lacy didn't budge while she waved a white envelope with heavy black writing on the outside. "It's from Paul."

Why would he write to her? A funny feeling planted an ice cube in Jonica's heart. She recognized the writing; it had adorned the only love letters she ever received.

"Really, Mrs. Duncan." She tried to laugh. "Are you trying to disrupt Paul and me just a week before our wedding?"

"There will be no wedding if you have the courage to read what Paul wrote to me."

Jonica flinched and saw the triumphant look in the watching blue eyes. She drew herself to her full five-foot, ten-inch dignity and stared at the slight woman. "I trust Paul Hamilton. Why should I read a letter he supposedly wrote? Can't you realize he stopped loving you years ago? If not, he would dump me and marry you, wouldn't he?"

"You little fool." Lacy's face mottled with anger. "Don't you want to know the truth? Can you marry him knowing he's still in love with another woman and always will be?"

The truth. Jonica though she knew it, yet if so, why hesitate? She took the letter, shook out the single page and scanned the bold writing she knew so well.

> *Dear Lacy,*
> *It's no use. The church would never go for it. Forget the whole idea; it won't work.*
> > *Paul*

"I tried to warn you," Lacy said. "Paul does love me but he's hesitating because he's afraid of what people will say." She preened. "I can make him come around, especially since there's no disgrace even among Christians in marrying a widow. I don't have a living husband and that's what held him back before. His father taught him to hate divorce." She laughed. "If you're as smart as everyone thinks you are, you won't stand in the way of Paul's happiness."

"You can never make him happy," Jonica cried, unwilling to accept the concrete evidence before her.

"Can you?" Lacy softly inquired. "In spite of professing to be a Christian, you're just a person from the other side of the tracks. I took the trouble to look you up. I have to hand it to you; you've come a long way from Slumville to Shepherd of Love but not far enough, Jonica Carr."

"You are evil," the tortured nurse whispered. "Get out."

Lacy's blue eyes darkened. "I can't see that going after the man you love and always have is evil but it doesn't make any difference now, does it?"

Jonica choked, feeling dirty all over, tainted with her past and smeared by this incredible, ugly scene. "Someday you'll be sorry." It sounded like an echo from childish threats at home. "You left your husband, came back here and pursued Paul—"

"And got him." Lacy started toward the door.

The petite woman's move steeled Jonica's determination not to give up without a fight. "Just a minute!" Her voice rang and her head came up. "You won't leave until I call Paul."

A curious glint in Lacy's eyes made her look like a cat. "Good idea." She perched on the arm of the couch.

The telephone at the Hamiltons rang three times. Four. Five. *Please, God, let me get Paul. If I can just hear his voice. . .*

"Hello?" A sleepy voice answered.

She sagged with relief. "Paul?" Her voice broke.

"Did you write a note to Lacy Duncan?" She held her breath.

An eternity later Paul said, "Yes, but how did you know? It was supposed to be confidential—"

She cradled the telephone before replacing it on the receiver.

"Well?" Lacy's question cracked like rotting ice.

Jonica looked at Lacy and licked her parched lips. The phone rang in the stillness. Again. Both women stared at it and Jonica refused to answer. After ten rings it stopped—and the silence beat into her ears like a dinner gong. Somehow she got Lacy out, refusing to say another word. She must get away. Paul would surely come to see why she hung up on him. Soon. She snatched a weekend case, crammed whatever clothes and personal effects she could grab the quickest, and stuffed it full. She dressed, ran to her car and put the case in the trunk, conscious of time passing with meteor-like speed. Chill air reminded her winter hadn't gone and she hurried back for her warm parka. Its down lining warmed her body but not her heart.

She experienced a moment of panic when the motor turned over but didn't catch. She hadn't used her car for several days. What if it didn't start? She tried again, it purred and Jonica drove out of the parking lot, away from Paul and the only real love she had ever known.

eight

Jonica's headlights made twin streams that pierced the murky February morning. She aimlessly followed the flow of traffic to I-5, merged and headed north. Fog and light rain grayed the day into nothingness. Exit after exit depleted the freeway as commuters headed toward work but Jonica kept on. When she reached Everett, she hesitate. Canada lay to the north but she had no desire to go there now. Behind her lay—she gripped the wheel until her gloved fingers ached. It didn't matter where she went, just that she got away. Perhaps someday she could return and behave in a civilized manner but not now. The healthy urge to wring Lacy Duncan's neck rose, then she remembered the hesitancy before Paul admitted his guilt.

"Forget it," she ordered. A large sign indicated a turnoff to Skykomish. She took it, crossed a long bridge, drove by the restored town and headed east on Highway 2. Not the best time of year to go through Stevens Pass but why not? Her all-weather tires were adequate unless a major storm came. "At least I have time off so I'm not letting the hospital down," she muttered, then a pang shot through her. What a far cry from the sleeping-in day she had promised herself to start her vacation and wedding preparations.

Sheer grit kept her alert for a time but before she reached Skykomish the weather had worsened and exhaustion threatened. She found a simple but spotless motel, ordered a takeout meal and forced herself to eat. To her utter amazement, she fell asleep the minute she crawled into the comfortable bed and when she awakened, a feeling of physical rest made her decide to go on over the Pass. Storm predictions on TV gave her a few qualms but she knew how to drive in northwest road conditions so gassed up and continued.

Skykomish disappeared from her rearview mirror, a charming town lightly dusted with snow. Ahead lay— what?

"If I've heard once, I've heard countless time that when You slam doors, God, You open others." Jonica tried to keep the agony from her heart. "Well, now's the time to prove it. Except You didn't slam the door shut. Paul did."

Bittersweet memories rode with her away into the growing snowstorm that spatted wet patches on her windshield, but the runaway nurse didn't care. The wilder the evening, the better. It matched her reckless mood and challenged her driving skills until she had nothing left to waste in mourning an untrue fiancé.

> ❧

Dr. Paul Hamilton disbelievingly listened to the dial tone in his ear, shook the telephone and pressed its redial button. The sound of angry bees buzzed. He hit the button again. This time he heard it ring. Three, five, ten times. "Impossible. Jonica couldn't have left her room between the time she hung up on me and I called back." Worry knitted his brows into a straight black line. "Why did she hang up in the first place?" He remembered the strain in her voice when she asked if he had written to Lacy, his own shock and stumbling answer. Disgust filled him. Why had he stuttered like an embarrassed school boy? No wonder she broke the connection. "I'd like to know what Lacy Jones-Duncan told her," he muttered, while dressing with quick movements. "On the other hand, what could she say? Why can't she get it into her head anything I ever felt for her is deader than last year's fallen leaves?" Thankful that his father and Emily had risen early and gone for a walk, he changed, then scribbled a hasty note, *Gone to see Jonica,* slid into a jacket against the morning chill and soon reached Shepherd of Love. Yet no amount of knocking roused Jonica. A sleepy Nancy Galbraith appeared a few minutes later, however, yawning and fastening a robe.

"Paul? Is something wrong?"

"I don't know. I got a strange call from Jonica, tried to call back and no one answered. Do you happen to know where she is? I doubt she could sleep through my knocking."

A little frown pencilled itself between Nancy's silky brows. "Come to think of it, I vaguely remember hearing her door close—twice—but I was too sleepy for it to register.

"Twice?" Then someone was with her?" Paul's jaw set. "You don't happen to know if it was Lacy Duncan, do you?"

Nancy shook her head and her dark eyes looked trouble. "I don't know but Lacy has been hanging around Jonica a lot lately."

"She's a spoiled troublemaker," Paul exclaimed. "Too bad someone doesn't teach her the lesson she should have had as a child." Satisfaction at the thought made him smile in spite of his nagging concern about Jonica.

"Maybe Jonica went over to the dining room," Nancy suggested. "Although she usually makes her own breakfast here."

"I'll look."

Paul sprinted down the hall, followed by Nancy's low call, "Good luck. I'll be praying."

He stopped and whirled back toward the watching nurse. "You think it's something serious?" he incredulously asked.

Nancy slowly shook her head but her eyes didn't brighten. "I just don't know. Usually Jonica is so tired when she gets off her shift she can't wait to shower and get to bed. It simply isn't like her to go out at this time of day." She glanced at her watch. "Better hurry if you mean to catch her. Breakfast is over in just a few moments."

One lightning glance at the deserted staff dining room sent Paul's heart plummeting. He forced himself to smile at one of the girls who was cleaning up and kept his voice casual. "Guess I missed Jonica."

"She didn't come in this morning, Doctor." The girl smiled. "You'll probably find her in her rooms if she isn't already asleep. Lindsey from Surgery said they had a rough night. I talked with her when she came in for breakfast."

"Thanks." Paul felt like a bloodhound sniffing out one clue one at a time. He curbed his first impulse—to rush to Lindsey Best's room and ask if she knew anything about Jonica. Her night would have been just as hectic. Besides, with Jonica off duty the next few weeks,

Lindsey and Emily and the other surgical personnel were going to be swamped. Not even to appease his need to find and talk with Jonica could he disturb the tired nurses' rest. He walked to the doctors' lounge, wrote a brief note asking Lindsey to call him when she read it, and prepared to wait. Unease accompanied him on the duties he forced himself to accomplish and when his pager summoned him late that afternoon, he could barely restrain his eagerness.

"Dr. Paul? You wanted me to contact you?"

He could visualize the puzzled look on the attractive red-headed nurse's face. He'd never before slipped a message under her door.

"Yes. I need to talk with you."

"I can meet you in our quarters' living room in a half-hour," Lindsey promised.

Rested-looking, freckles shining and face scrubbed, she appeared five minutes before her set time. "Is something wrong?"

He hesitated, unwilling to stir up anything, yet driven by an inner feeling all was not well. He had periodically checked Jonica's room and the staff parking lot during the day and found no trace of her. "Did anything special go wrong on shift last night?"

"No-o. Busier than usual, but nothing extraordinary. Why?"

He matched her forthrightness with his own and gave her the same carefully thought-out story he'd told Nancy Galbraith. "Jonica called me maybe an hour after she got off duty. She sounded, well, strange."

A flood of angry color came to Lindsey's face and her brown eyes flashed. "I'll bet it was *her* doing."

"Who?"

"The witch." She flushed. "Sorry, that isn't a nice thing for a Christian to say but she makes me so mad, coming around smoother than whipped cream and digging her painted claws into Jonica all the time. Never anything anyone can pounce on but little innuendoes and—"

"And reminders we were once engaged." Paul struggled with hatred for the albatross Lacy was around his neck. "By any chance, was she here this morning?"

"Was she!" Indignation raised Lindsey's voice and she mimicked the older woman to perfection. " 'Jonica, answer the door. It's Lacy.' A lot she cared that Jonica and I both had Do Not Disturb signs on our doors. I wasn't eavesdroping, either. Even our good acoustics didn't drown out Mrs. Duncan's knocking. I opened my door a crack, planning to tell her we'd had a really bad night." She broke off.

"Did you hear anything else?" Paul leaned forward. "I'm not asking because I'm curious. It's just that Jonica seems to have gone off somewhere and isn't back."

Concern erased Lindsey's natural aversion to gossip. "Lacy said in a kind of excited voice, 'This won't take long and it can't wait. All this time I've held back but . . .' I realized the conversation was going to be personal and shut my door. I must have drowsed because later I heard the door close—twice." She sighed. "I wish now I'd barged in and thrown Her Nibs out. Jonica is too special a person to be tormented."

"Yes, she is," the young doctor soberly agreed. "Lindsey do you think she would resent it if you just stepped inside her room and looked around? She doesn't lock the inside door, does she?"

"No. None of us do. We all have keys to the door from the covered passage to this living room so leaving our own doors unlocked is perfectly safe." She shook her head. "If you think it's all right, I'll look."

They slowly walked down the long hall to the suite at the end. Lindsey turned the knob of Jonica's bed-sitting room and pushed the door inward. She gasped. "My goodness, she must have left in a hurry. Jonica never leaves her clothes strewn about like some of the rest of us."

Dismayed, Paul could only stare. The closed doors gaped open. A dress sagged from a hanger; a uniform lay crumpled in a corner. "Is anything gone?"

"Hmmm." Lindsey's observing gaze surveyed the disorder. "Her down-filled parka, heavy slacks and shoes." She shrugged. "I can't tell what else."

"Check her dressing table, please."

Lindsey reported, after a cursory glance there and into the bathroom, "Toilet articles missing." She turned a sympathetic glance toward Paul. "She evidently plans to be gone for a few days."

Or more. But he wouldn't let his fear surface. "Lindsey, I want you to stay here long enough for me to make a call. I want a witness." He could see the shock in her face, although she nodded understandingly. It took but a moment to look up Lacy Jones-Duncan's number. "This is Dr. Hamilton. Please let me speak with Mrs. Duncan."

"Certainly." The well-trained servant added, "Just a moment, please," yet far more than moments passed before he returned. "I'm sorry but madam has left orders not to be disturbed."

Paul choked back anger and thanked the servant. He cradled the phone and told Lindsey, "She's going to be disturbed, all right. I still need a witness, though."

Lindsey looked stricken. "I'm sorry, but it's quite a distance to the Duncan mansion and I have to go on duty." She brightened. "Wait just a minute." Lindsey loped out the open door and knocked on the one next door. "Nancy?"

"Yes?" The off-duty nurse appeared. Her soft rose skirt and sweater highlighted her dark hair and eyes.

"Dr. Paul needs you," Lindsey said simply. "I can't get released from duty tonight and he has an errand to run that needs a witness. Can you go?"

"Of course." Not a moment's hesitation or demand for an explanation preceded her quick assent.

"Good. He will explain." Lindsey smiled and headed off down the hall.

In terse sentences Paul reported what Lindsey had seen and heard. "I have to find Jonica. I don't know what Mrs. Duncan has done but it evidently sent Jonica into a spin. Lacy refused to accept my call. I'm going out there and get the truth. Are you game?"

"Absolutely. I'll just get a jacket." She vanished and reappeared clad in a warm jacket that matched her skirt and sweater. "Jonica is so vulnerable in spite of all her efficiency. Sometimes I see myself in her."

Paul saw the pain in Nancy's eyes and deliberated whether he should give her an opening to talk. She forestalled him by adding, "The wedding is so close, I hoped she could get through before anyone planted doubts in her mind."

"Doubts of my love? That's hard to believe." Paul helped her into his Accord, slid into the driver's seat and fastened his seat belt. "I love her second only to our Lord."

Nancy slowly said, "I'm more concerned about Jonica doubting herself than you. She doesn't have a lot of self-esteem."

Again Paul felt the nurse hovered on the verge of saying more but Nancy changed the subject.

"I won't be surprised to find that Mrs. Duncan isn't home."

"She'd better be," Paul grimly told her.

All his grimness availed nothing. A frankly surprised butler met them at the door when they reached the Duncan mansion with the news that Mrs. Jones-Duncan had suddenly decided to fly to California. "I'm sorry, Doctor." He shook his head. "I don't think she had planned to go but shortly after you called, she summoned me and said she didn't know when she'd be back."

"Did she by any chance leave a message for me?" Paul held a faint hope that died when the butler shook his head. No. She had a maid pack and the chauffeur drove her to Sea-Tac International. An interview with the chauffeur elicited no further information. Yes, he had driven his employer to the airport. No, she had given no hint as to either her destination or when she would return.

"If I hear from her, would you want me to let you know?" the helpful butler asked.

"Very much." Paul turned away with a wide-eyed Nancy right behind him, concern written all over her smooth face.

"Now what?" he despairingly asked when they were back in the car. "Nancy, she is closer to you than to the others, although she likes them and I know they return the feeling. What is she likely to do?" He stared into the drizzle from massed dark clouds and made no move to start the motor.

Nancy didn't speak for a long time. At last she said, "Something has hurt her. Badly. We can be reasonably sure it came from her morning caller, who is incommunicado. She doesn't talk a lot about her childhood but I know when things got too bad at home she fled. Perhaps she is doing the same now, seeking shelter and time to think." She stopped then asked, "Do you know what Lacy Duncan might have said or done?"

"I suspect that she twisted the truth or lied outright in the hopes of doing mischief." A little bitterness crept into him. "I can't understand why Jonica didn't have more trust in me, no matter what Lacy said. She should know I would never do anything to hurt her."

"It is almost impossible to trust when life has hurt you deeply."

All through the silent drive back to the hospital and the next few days Paul remembered Nancy's comment. Why hadn't he been more sensitive? He'd thought his surrounding love could blot out Jonica's years of struggle, living in a false hope. What she needed was a deeper relationship with Christ. Until it came, Jonica Carr would continue to be prey to doubt of self and others.

"Perhaps she will find a place to hide and think," Nancy said several days later when no trace of the runaway nurse had been found. For Jonica's sake, her close friends had kept her absence downplayed. Paul surreptitiously consulted a friend on the police force and used a "case study" approach.

"It isn't a police matter, the way I see it," his friend advised. "There's no evidence of foul play. The woman you mention had time off coming. So it wasn't considerate of her to leave without letting someone know her destination. People don't always do what they should."

On the 13th of February, Paul, his father and Emily, Nancy and the minister who had been going to perform the wedding met for consultation. "Is there any chance she will come back and just be in the Chapel at the time set?" the pastor wanted to know.

"I don't think so." Paul felt as haggard as his mirror showed he had grown. "I can't help believing she's in real trouble but I don't know what it is. If only we knew where she is!" He gripped his fingers into fists.

"I think so, too," Nancy offered in her soft voice. "No matter how she felt, I don't think Jonica would allow the wedding to stand and not show up. Her sense of duty is so high it would be impossible for her to do such a thing."

The minister shook his head. "Then we'd better cancel the arrangements; just say they have been postponed."

Valentine's Day dawned overcast and murky. A little snow spitefully mingled with heavy rain. Weather forecasts told of exulting ski lodges that welcomed continuing falls of fresh snow on top of an already-good pack.

Paul stared out the living room window of his home,

glad that Dad and Emily had insisted he continue to live with them for the present. The thought of rattling around in the tastefully furnished apartment he had leased until he and Jonica decided where to buy or build was more than he could handle. He had ordered the apartment repainted in her favorite colors: blues, greens, a vivid thrust of brighter colors here and there. When finished, he'd refused to let her see it, anticipating carrying her across the threshold in the time-honored tradition and dedicating their first home to God and each other.

Now—desolation. What had red hearts, foil-wrapped boxes of candy bearing enormous ribbons and fat cupids to do with his loss? "God, where is she?" he prayed. "Please, wherever it may be, take care of her. Help her and heal her. If it be Your will, bring her back safely." He took a deep breath. "Most of all, fill her heart with Your Spirit that she may know even though others let her down, You never will."

Refreshed by the time with his Lord, Paul forced himself back to the plans for the Shepherd of Love Sanctuary. Even his personal travail couldn't slow the relentless progress of the project that would benefit so many. Yet again and again the sad-hearted doctor found his attention wandering. A wall clock ticked seconds into minutes, its cadence demanding, *Where is Jon-i-ca? Where is Jon-i-ca?* but Dr. Hamilton had no answer. Just a hundred disturbing questions. How could even a Lacy Jones-Duncan have made anything out of the only note Paul had written to her in more than ten years? Why had Jonica believed whatever she'd been told? And the final, hurtful question he couldn't overcome—

if she had so little trust in him, could they ever have the kind of marriage he wanted? Or would their house be built on the sand of her uncertainty, only to crumble when life's storms pounded against it.

nine

"Paul." Peter Hamilton's troubled voice broke into his son's sea of turmoil. "It's time to file a missing persons report."

Paul shoved his chair back from the desk that overflowed with paperwork needing his attention. "I know. I've held off until today hoping she'd come back or call. Our wedding day. What a farce. I'm here worried sick and only God knows where she is, fighting battles we can only imagine!"

"Steady, boy." Love shone in the dark eyes that looked so like his son's. "God *does* know where she is and we can take comfort from that."

Paul stood, went to the window and blindly stared across the sodden lawn. "Sometimes I wonder. There are so many crazies out there. What if one of them has her?" Fear hoarsened his voice.

Peter came to his son and put his arm around the sagging shoulders. "All we can do is trust God," he reminded. "There are a dozen reasons we haven't heard from her. Still, let's go file a report. Better get Nancy or Lindsey to give you as accurate a list as possible of what she wore and took."

It seemed pitifully sketchy when they presented it to a hardfaced officer whose kind eyes looked strange in such a time-worn setting. In a surprisingly soft voice, he took the information and promised to get it out immediately. He also suggested that TV and radio be alerted, with the request that if anyone had seen the missing nurse, they contact the police. "You'll get a lot of bad leads," he warned. "People who think any tall woman wearing a parka is your fiancee. On the other hand, we may get a decent clue or two."

Paul felt comforted by the man's efficiency but when the predicted "sightings" began coming in, he wondered if the callers were making them up or if ninety percent of the women in Seattle were tall, attractive and wearing parkas.

One caller insisted he had seen Jonica in deep conversation with a pilot at the airport who took off in his own plane. No, he didn't see the woman get in but she could have. He'd looked away, then back just in time to see the plane taxiing down the runway. He grew voluble about the plane. "Prettiest little bird I ever saw. Green as a shamrock and trimmed with the whitest white."

"Anything else?" Paul marveled at the patience of the officer who screened the calls and personally interviewed those that might be true, as in this case.

The eager man wrinkled his forehead. "Uh, yes. He had something painted on the side—a design. Kind of strange looking. A cloud, with a cross painted on it."

Paul's mouth fell open. Excitement quivered in him. "I know that plane. It belongs to Garry Sterling, a friend of mine."

Phone lines crackled. Paul clenched his hands. Had Jonica for some reason boarded Garry's plane? But why? She barely knew the pilot; he'd come to their table once when by chance they dined at the same restaurant.

The helpful officer grunted into the phone, listened, grunted again. He slowly replaced it. "Sorry, Dr. Hamilton. I have more bad news for you. Mr. Sterling's plane crashed over a week ago, in fact, the very day you say Miss Carr disappeared." His face worked. "Tough luck."

"Is Garry all right?" Paul prepared himself for the worst.

"He's in a coma at Harborview."

"So we have no way of knowing whether Jonica was on the plane?"

"Just a second." He dialed, waited, barked into the phone, "Any sign of a passenger in the Sterling wreck?"

Paul's nerves screamed in the silence.

"Plane too busted up to tell, huh. Okay. Thanks." He turned back to Paul. "The way I see it, Sterling's your best hope. You know the doctors at Harborview, don't you? Go see when Sterling's going to come out of the coma, if he is. He's the only one who can tell you if he had a passenger."

"If I didn't know God is in control of this world and not a capricious Fate, I'd swear there's a conspiracy against our finding Jonica," Paul told his father and Emily later that evening. A visit to Harborview had netted both encouraging and discouraging information. Garry Sterling had begun to show signs of consciousness. Perhaps in a day or two he would be able to answer questions. Yet his doctors made no promises.

"You know how it is," one told Paul. "The only predictable thing about comas is their unpredictable nature." With that, Paul had to be content. He requested that they let him know as soon as a change for the better occurred and dragged home, not knowing whether to be glad or sorry.

The worst news lay in the terrain where the plane had gone down, a rugged area in the North Cascades. If Jonica had been aboard, if she had been thrown clear and escaped harm, if she had survived the mountain storms, miles lay between her and help. Sterling had been off course. The rescue team who had helicoptered him out had no suspicion of a passenger's presence. When Garry failed to arrive at Bellingham on time, a reconnaissance flight spotted him from the air. He'd been rescued just before another storm swooped down.

Four days limped by. The hospital now knew the whole story. Compassion for Jonica and Dr. Hamilton shone in every face. Special prayer services were scheduled in the Chapel. Nancy, Lindsey, Patty and Shina's natural gaiety only surfaced when working with patients who needed them. Nicholas Fairchild and the Hospital Director, all those involved in the Sanctuary project, Peter and Emily strove to lift Paul's dread. One night he cried out to God, "Please, if I could just know."

The next morning Harborview called. "Dr. Hamilton? Your friend Garry Sterling is awake. Give him a few hours and you can see him for just a minute, but don't disturb him."

Paul set his lips and obeyed. Long years of repression in the face of tragedy put a forced lilt in his voice when he wrung Garry's hand and said, "God sure was watching over you, old man. Say, good thing you didn't have a passenger, right?" He felt he'd suffocate before Garry smiled and nodded.

"Right. The passenger seat got it worse than I did." Garry stirred restlessly, eyes still dull.

"I'll come again when you get your sleep out," Paul told him and slipped away, relieved yet more puzzled than ever. The lead, like others, had proved false. Thank God for that! Yet, where was Jonica? How could the earth open up and swallow her so completely? Only the faith that God still held her in His capable hands gave Paul the strength to go on.

That night, the dedicated police officer called. "Dr. Hamilton? We have a real clue. A Jonica Carr that matches your description spent the night of February 7 at a motel in Skykomish. Well, sort of."

"What do you mean?" Paul gripped the phone.

"She checked in early, before noon. The motel owner said she normally didn't let anyone in that time of day but Miss Carr looked so tired she made an exception. Something funny, though. She doesn't know when Miss Carr left. It could have even been in late afternoon or early evening. What with some snow and being busy, she didn't pay a lot of attention until about nine that night when she noticed the car was gone. She still didn't think much about it. People come and go at odd hours. The next morning she slept in, then found the unit empty when she went to clean."

"So she can't say for certain if Jonica went out to eat, came back and slept, or if she left the night before."

"That's right." The officer sounded sympathetic. "Nice enough woman. Didn't think much about it 'cause she gets all kinds. Then when Miss Carr's picture appeared in the newspaper she started wondering and called. I had her repeat the whole thing over again but there wasn't anything else and she has no idea which way Miss Carr intended to travel. I'd guess over Stevens Pass, except the owner said a bad storm swept through that night. Think your nurse would take off over a mountain in the middle of a storm?"

"I honestly don't know. I hope not."

"So do I," the officer ponderously said. "Skykomish ended up with a foot of fresh snow and the pass is a whale of a lot higher."

New fear spurted in Paul's heart. "If there had been an accident, wouldn't someone know?"

"It's been known to happen that accidents sometimes happen when no other cars or trucks are around," the disembodied voice warned. "In a heavy snow, drivers are watching the road and not signs of tracks. Besides, there's always the danger of avalanches."

Oh, God, was Jonica buried somewhere under tons of fallen snow? Paul's hands, so steady when performing even the most delicate surgery, shook like aspen leaves in a storm.

"What do we do now?"

"I've already contacted Highway Patrol and the Leavenworth Police. Now we wait." The gruff voice stopped. "Uh, I understand you pray a lot. This is a good time. I just wish I had better news for you. This doesn't mean Miss Carr isn't all right. It does mean we have an idea of where she was and her probable destination. I'll keep in touch."

"Thank you," came through colorless lips. Paul buried his face in his hands and groaned. Instead of reassuring him, the detailed report had raised dozens of new fears, new visions of a terrified Jonica clinging to the wheel of her car; oceans of falling snow, enveloping, drowning. Death, instantaneous or slow. The lowering of body temperature. Oblivion. Paul clutched his trust in God and began to pray. . .

❧

Jonica Carr left Skykomish behind and with it, some of her misery. Stevens Pass, especially in a growing storm, was no place for daydreaming. Scenic and beautiful, it didn't offer the wider highway that I-90 over Snoqualmie Pass boasted. Neither did it have as much friendly traffic. Truckers chose the faster way when possible and tonight only a few vehicles came toward her, their lights ghostly in the softly falling snow.

"I hope that I don't get into a chains-required situation," she worried, anxiously watching the snowfall. "If I can reach the summit and start down the other side, I'll be okay." Gloved hands firm on the wheel, she expertly guided her car through slush. Not once did she consider turning back. She never had. Even at fifteen, when caring for herself looked impossible, when she felt at the end of her proverbial rope, she somehow tied a knot and hung on by sheer grit.

A long time later she breathed a sigh of relief and passed the summit, noticing the few cars and trucks sitting in the snow. Loneliness assailed her once she left the lights of the buildings behind. Traffic had all but stopped. Still she kept on. If all went well, she could be in Leavenworth by midnight, even under the present road conditions.

With one of the strange quirks life holds in store, Jonica had just sighed with relief, knowing she had all but conquered the mountain when it happened. Above the keening storm a low rumble began. Northwest-trained, she recognized immediately what it was. She slowed, looked up. Above her a great ledge of snow shifted, gained momentum. Jonica slammed the gas pedal to the floor. Her car leaped ahead. Yet she knew she could not outrun the length of snow wall rushing down.

"God, if You're here, help me!" she screamed. She glanced to her right, away from the menace, and flicked her headlights to high beam. Instead of the steep drop from the highway most of the road had, a more gentle slope lay below her.

In the split second of decision, she knew her only hope lay in that slope. In seconds, the slide would cover the roadway and her car if she remained where she was. Going over the edge might prove fatal but she had no choice. A slim possibility existed that the wall of snow would pile up and not spill over to bury her. Would the momentum of her car carry her far enough down for that to happen? She had to chance it. Setting her teeth in her bottom lip, she jerked the wheel to the right, glad for the speed she had gained. Down, down the car went with Jonica braced against the seat and relentlessly holding the gas pedal to the floor.

She sobbed as the snow-covered slope slowed her progress, wheels churning against the white peril. A gigantic fir loomed before her. She spun the wheel to the left. The snow-clogged wheels could not respond fast enough. In horror, Jonica saw the tree grow larger. In moments her car would crash into it head-on. "God, this is it." She flung open the door, released her seat belt and jumped. . . .

"Cold. So cold." Jonica curled into a ball. Had the heating system in her room malfunctioned? She reached to pull her blankets higher and couldn't find them. Her eyes opened. Had she gone blind? Her room never got this dark. Even in the wee hours a little light filtered in from the illuminated hospital grounds.

She sat up and flung out both hands. Her dazed brain refused to comprehend until in stretching, her parka sleeves pulled up and away from her gloves. The impact of snow on her bare wrists cleared her mind and everything came back—her flight, the slide, her wild plunge over the edge of the bank. She also grew aware of a weight of snow on her body and huge flakes beating down on her. "Thank You, God, that I'm alive," she whispered. "Now what?'

Jonica struggled to her feet and brushed away the snow. A glimpse at her watch told her she'd been unconscious for more than an hour. She shivered, remembering how she'd run back for her parka at the last minute when leaving Shepherd of Love. Where was the car? Could she find it in the storm? If only she could tell which direction she faced, but the snow made it impossible.

"I can't panic," she said and her voice came back to her, muffled by the storm. "All I have to do is climb up to the highway and keep walking down. A road crew will find me. Which way is up?" She stamped her feet until feeling came back into them, deeply grateful she had even awakened. Had God touched her shoulder or spirit that she might live?

She set out determinedly, but found that the ground soon sloped down. She reversed herself and rejoiced. Although snow swirled to her knees and made every step a chore, the exercise warmed her blood and made it race through her veins. Jonica laughed—and she thrilled to her height and weight. Suppose she were Lacy Duncan's size? She'd never make it through this ordeal. Somehow the malicious woman's importance faded when stacked up against the necessity of fighting for her life. Hands outstretched so she wouldn't walk smack into a tree, the runaway nurse stumbled into black night, not realizing she climbed a rise that led away from the road and not back to it.

Even her superb stamina faltered by the time her watch said four o'clock. If she could only rest. "No!" she shouted. "That's how people die." She drove herself on until a little light behind the snow and her watch said morning crept near. Still she staggered through the deepening snow. Feet and legs had long since gone numb. Her medical training warned that hypothermia came closer all the time.

Jonica raised her foot to take a step, lost her balance and tried to regain it. The heavy snow beneath her feet slid and she realized she had gained the top of something—a hill— a rise. The next instant she fell heavily, automatically throwing her arms in front of her face to protect it. Like a tobogganing child, she gathered speed. Her parka protected her chest and the snow hid sharp stones that could have ripped open her slacks and knees.

Heartbeats or an eternity later she slowed and stopped. A rapid check showed no broken bones but one ankle had twisted and she knew it would swell. She strained her eyes—and saw nothing but more snow. Gloom surrounded her, a strange gray and white world that held no mercy. If only there were light she could cope. This terrible murk depressed her and prevented seeing what lay ahead, behind or to either side.

"God, are You here? I need You." Jonica stumbled to her feet and took a limping step forward. Pain sprayed through her right ankle. She gritted her teeth and took another step. What was the use of damaging herself further when she didn't even know which way to go? She closed her eyes and in spite of her best efforts, a single tear slipped out. She thought of Paul, the man she loved but hadn't trusted; of her friends at Shepherd of Love. Her mind wandered, back to the day she reported for duty. An electric current surged through her body, the knowledge she held a key in her mind that would unlock the answer to her dilemma. She concentrated, harder even than when she took the hardest tests to gain her coveted BS degree in Nursing. If she could only remember. Forcing herself to go back to the moment she walked down the hall to the Director's office, Jonica halted outside the door. "That's it." Words, engraved on the door, a strange inscription for a hospital director's office.

Thy word is a lamp unto my feet, and a light unto my path.

Chilled from the storm, miserable and aching, yet the words brought a ray of hope. "God," she cried. "Please, be my lamp in this awful darkness. I have to tell Paul—" What? For the first time she realized how her head pounded. She must have struck it when she hurled herself from the car. New fear gripped her. If she had a concussion and passed out, it meant death.

Jonica set her jaw and took another limping step, avoiding young snow-covered trees and low bushes that threatened to snatch her. She paused. Could she break a branch and use it for a crude crutch? It would take some of the weight from her injured ankle. She paused by a tree, shook snow from a branch and gripped it with strong hands. It didn't budge. She tried again with the same results.

"You stubborn branch. I'm going to break you," she told the sturdy tree. Grabbing it with both hands she pulled her feet up from the ground and let her full 150 pounds hang dead weight. The branch creaked ominously. Jonica put her good foot down, bent her knee, gave a little spring that sent her off the ground again. A splintering of wood warned her just in time. She quickly put her feet down again and tugged, hard. The branch broke close to the trunk of the tree and hung by a single strip of bark. Jonica yanked it free, struggled until she could get some of the bushy branches off and triumphantly held up her homemade crutch. Now if she just knew which way to go.

Using the tree branch for support, she made it to the top of a nearby swell of ground and surveyed the vast, trackless scene that blurred with snow and low-hanging fog, turning in a complete circle, heart sinking. She froze and strained her eyes. Could that be the pale sun off to her right? If so, it meant she had been traveling in the wrong direction for hours. The light remained steady, smaller surely than sunlight, even if partially screened by the snow that no longer came so thickly but still fell. Did someone *live* out here?

"A light unto my path." The weary nurse turned her face toward the glow and set off again, grimacing when her right foot came down too heavily but never taking her gaze from the tiny beacon somewhere in the elusive distance.

ten

Paul Hamilton sometimes felt himself to be a classic case of dual personality. One side of him coolly executed the hundred and more details concerned with the establishment of the Shepherd of Love Sanctuary. The other half quivered and waited while minutes lagged into hours. The startling news that Jonica had stayed overnight in Skykomish had raised his hopes. Yet they dead-ended when no further trace of her could be found. Some clever research by the police did turn up an interesting fact. Highway 2 had suffered a slide across the road the same night Jonica supposedly traveled it, resulting in a closure for a full day while crews cleared it.

"Why so long?" Paul demanded. "I thought those graders were out all night in bad weather."

"That's the trouble. The snow kept coming down so hard it hampered getting the slide cleared," he was told.

"I suppose they checked to make sure no one got caught in it."

His policeman friend nodded. "Sure did. Found nothing out of the ordinary." He scratched his cheek thoughtfully. "Only trouble is—it snowed so hard they wouldn't have been able to learn much."

"Dr. Hamilton, now that we're pretty sure your fiancee took that road, and since Leavenworth reports no sign of her, Search and Rescue will be out there looking and they carry real fine tooth combs."

Paul whirled. "Why didn't the motelkeeper know Jonica was missing sooner?"

The policeman shrugged. "She says she 'ain't much hand for TV and had been too busy to read the papers.' I guess she had them stacked in a pile and when she got around to reading them, called us."

"I think I'll go up there and see if I can find anything," Paul murmured.

"Don't. You'll get in the way. Search and Rescue know what they're doing. Let them do it."

The following day news came. Paul didn't know whether to let himself hope or sink in despair when he learned what the valiant crew had found—Jonica's car at the bottom of a slope, overturned and empty, hidden from the road above because of the heavy snow that had blanketed it and erased all sign of tracks over the edge.

"If she's wandering around out there they'll find her." The policeman's eyes showed disbelief that it would happen. He scratched at his cheek again. "If she wasn't too bad hurt, though, seems like she'd have walked out, 'cept the Weather Bureau reminded me how low fog and continuing snow kept visibility really poor the next day."

Paul turned to his only remaining source of comfort. "God, it looks hopeless. Yet You can move mountains. Now we need to find Jonica, regardless of what happened." He also decided that if no word came, he'd go look for her himself, regardless of disapproval. That afternoon when the phone rang, he raced to it, dreading possible bad news. Lacy Duncan's voice rang in his ear.

"I have to see you. I just got home from California and heard that Jonica Carr is missing."

"What can you possibly care?"

A little choking sound at the other end of the wire preceded a broken, "Please, Paul. I didn't mean for anything like this to happen."

Could it be a trap? Paul had to take the chance. An hour later he was ushered into Lacy's mansion. Red-eyed, without makeup, the small woman looked shriveled. She motioned Paul to a chair across from hers in front of the shining white fireplace. He hadn't seen her so messy since cheerleading days when she forgot her looks in the interest of leading yells. "Have they found her? Paul, she isn't dead, is she? I can't stand it. I never knew she would. . ." Her voice died.

He found himself repeating the question he had asked over the phone, voice harsh. "What can you possibly care?"

Lacy sobbed and dabbed at her eyes with a tissue. "I thought if she broke the engagement you'd come back to me, so I showed her the note you wrote to me."

"Note! How could you make her believe what I told you about the church never consenting to hold that benefit dance you wanted to sponsor had anything to do with us? Any of us?"

Shame sent dark red streaks into the fair skin. "I-I said you were holding back because I'd been divorced; that you were afraid of what the church would think."

He looked at her as if she were the serpent who once tempted Eve. "You told Jonica Carr that?" Fury raged. He wanted to grab her slender shoulders and shake the living daylights out of her. "Lacy Duncan, it would

A Letter To Our Readers

Dear Reader:

In order that we might better contribute to your reading enjoyment, we would appreciate your taking a few minutes to respond to the following questions. When completed, please return to the following:

Rebecca Germany, Editor
Heartsong Presents
P.O. Box 719
Uhrichsville, Ohio 44683

1. Did you enjoy reading *Lamp in Darkness*?
   ☐ Very much. I would like to see more books
      by this author!
   ☐ Moderately
      I would have enjoyed it more if _____

   _____

2. Are you a member of *Heartsong Presents*? Yes   No
   If no, where did you purchase this book? _____

   _____

3. What influenced your decision to purchase
   this book? (Check those that apply.)

   ☐ Cover   ☐ Back cover copy

   ☐ Title   ☐ Friends

   ☐ Publicity   ☐ Other _____

4. On a scale from 1 (poor) to 10 (superior), please rate the following elements.

    ___Heroine   ___Plot

    ___Hero   ___Inspirational theme

    ___Setting   ___Secondary characters

5. What settings would you like to see covered in *Heartsong Presents* books?

    _____

    _____

6. What are some inspirational themes you would like to see treated in future books?_____

    _____

    _____

7. Would you be interested in reading other *Heartsong Presents* titles?   ❏ Yes   ❏ No

8. Please circle your age range:
  ❏ Under 18   ❏ 18-24   ❏ 25-34
  ❏ 35-45   ❏ 46-55   ❏ Over 55

9. How many hours per week do you read? _____

Name _____

Occupation _____

Address _____

City _____ State _____ Zip _____

Rocky Bluff Chronicles/Book Two

Contagious Love

A Sequel to Autumn Love

By Ann Bell

Whatever happened to the simple, happy days of Rocky Bluff?

Edith Harkness Dutton feels those days are gone forever, and
with good reason. Despite the promise of Edith's joyous second
marriage to Roy Dutton in the autumn of her life, life in this
Montana hamlet is anything but blissful.

A former standout high school basketball star abuses his wife
and is now stalking her despite a court-imposed restraining
order. . .Edith's son, Bob Harkness, struggles desperately to
save the family hardware store from bankruptcy only to watch
it go up in flames. . .and Roy always seems more tired than he
should.

As these seemingly isolated events entwine, Edith is drawn
into a maelstrom of emotions and needs. Never before have her
unwavering faith and contagious love been in such demand.
HP89

...Hearts ❤ng ......

...... Presents ......

Great Inspirational Romance at a Great Price!

Heartsong Presents books are inspirational romances in contemporary and historical settings, designed to give you an enjoyable, spirit-lifting reading experience. You can choose from 88 wonderfully written titles from some of today's best authors like Colleen L. Reece, Brenda Bancroft, Janelle Jamison, and many others.

When ordering quantities less than twelve, above titles are $2.95 each.

SEND TO: Heartsong Presents Reader's Service
P.O. Box 719, Uhrichsville, Ohio 44683

Please send me the items checked above. I am enclosing $_____
(please add $1.00 to cover postage per order. OH add 6.5% tax. PA and NJ add 6%.). Send check or money order, no cash or C.O.D.s, please.
To place a credit card order, call 1-800-847-8270.

NAME _____

ADDRESS _____

CITY/STATE _____ ZIP _____

HPS AUGUST

LOVE A GREAT LOVE STORY?

Introducing Heartsong Presents —
                                 Your Inspirational Book Club

Heartsong Presents Christian romance reader's service will provide you with four never before published romance titles every month! In fact, your books will be mailed to you at the same time advance copies are sent to book reviewers. You'll preview each of these new and unabridged books before they are released to the general public.

These books are filled with the kind of stories you have been longing for—stories of courtship, chivalry, honor, and virtue. Strong characters and riveting plot lines will make you want to read on and on. Romance is not dead, and each of these romantic tales will remind you that Christian faith is still the vital ingredient in an intimate relationship filled with true love and honest devotion.

Sign up today to receive your first set. Send no money now. We'll bill you only $9.97 post-paid with your shipment. Then every month you'll automatically receive the latest four "hot off the press" titles for the same low post-paid price of $9.97. That's a savings of 50% off the $4.95 cover price. When you consider the exaggerated shipping charges of other book clubs, your savings are even greater!

THERE IS NO RISK—you may cancel at any time without obligation. And if you aren't completely satisfied with any selection, return it for an immediate refund.

TO JOIN, just complete the coupon below, mail it today, and get ready for hours of wholesome entertainment.

Now you can curl up, relax, and enjoy some great reading full of the warmhearted spirit of romance.

take a handwritten message from God to make me ever come back to you."

"Don't, oh, don't." She held out one hand as if to ward off his anger. "Paul, if she dies, will it be my fault? God, what have I done?" Fear made her voice tremble.

Her instinctive cry to her Maker stilled Paul's scathing denouncement. "You had better ask God for forgiveness, Lacy," he said in a dull voice. "Jonica is in His hands now. There's nothing either one of us can do." He started for the door then glanced back at the crumpled figure in the expensive room where luxury reigned and peace had no place.

"Can you ever forgive me?" She raised her mottled face and whispered the request.

"I'm not the one you have sinned against. Someday, I hope you have the opportunity to ask Jonica's forgiveness." His voice broke and he blindly walked to the door while Lacy's cries rang in his ears. . .

20

Had she been walking forever? Jonica stumped through the snow, heartsick when she lost sight of the dim light somewhere ahead, encouraged when she saw it again. She no longer felt cold, but hot. Burning hot. *Left. Right. Left. Right.* Memory replaced her surroundings. She was the girl she had once been, stealing from a house that had never been a home, into the night, more frightened of what lay behind her than anything she might encounter. The look in her stepfather's eyes warned that even Jonica's mother couldn't protect the girl much longer. She shuddered in sympathy with the terrified teenager who escaped, but at great emotional cost.

Physically unharmed, she knew she carried scars that affected her outlook on life. Those scars had made her distrust Paul when presented with what appeared undeniable evidence of his faithlessness.

Why hadn't she given him a chance to explain? If only she had answered the ringing telephone—was it only yesterday—she wouldn't be lost, alone, hurt.

Her guiding light flickered and she panicked. "God, please, don't let it go out before I get there!" she cried and tried to hurry. She knew she'd almost reached the end of her stamina. The rude crutch dug into her side when she leaned more and more heavily on it. It proved awkward and several times she fell in the deep snow. Finally she came to a clump of small trees, parted the branches and rejoiced. The light shone brighter and through the gloom she could see the dark outline of a building—a cabin, maybe, or a hut. With the last of her strength she painfully made her way to the single step, limped across a covered porch and beat on the door. "Please, let me in."

At first she received no answer. She pounded and called again. This time a feeble, "Come in," rewarded her efforts. Jonica pushed open the unlocked door. If she lived to be older than Methuselah she would never forget what she saw. First, a small wood heater, warmly glowing. She dropped her tree limb and dragged herself toward it, conscious that her former feeling of heat had changed to shaking chills. She stripped off her soaked gloves, stained with pitch, and held her hands out to the warmth. At the same time, the weak voice said, "Thank God you've come!" and she turned toward a bunk bed in the corner. Her shocked gaze

took in the last thing one would imagine finding in a snowbound cabin: an elderly woman propped up in the bottom bunk bed, salt-and-pepper hair disarrayed, dull eyes enormous in a white face.

"Why, who are you? What are you doing here?" Jonica gasped.

"Sarah Milligan. I—"

Her visitor's legs gave way and she sank to the floor, barely conscious of her surroundings. "Tired. So tired."

"Can you get into the top bunk?" Sarah's voice penetrated the fog Jonica knew would soon claim her completely. She managed to shake her head no, the smothering grayness obliterated everything except the need for sleep.

Nightmares followed. Friends and enemies danced in and out of her feverish mind. Sometimes she threw off blankets that reminded her of the heavy snow pressing her down. At other times she curled into a ball and her teeth chattered, neither knowing nor caring where she was. Once she surfaced and asked, "Who are you?" to the strange woman who held a cold cloth to her forehead, but dropped back into oblivion before she learned the answer.

When Jonica at last regained consciousness, the warm room lay quiet and peaceful around her. She occupied the lower bunk bed. Nearby, the woman who had bid her come in, nodded in a rocker. Gradually, the nurse's mind cleared. She surveyed the cabin's interior, noting how clean and cozy it was. Her eyes widened at a neat pile of blankets on the floor. Shame scorched her. Sarah Milligan must somehow have put her stranger guest in her own bed and slept on the floor.

"How long have I been here?" Jonica asked when the older woman opened her eyes and smiled.

"Three days." Sarah slowly stood, walked to the stove, filled a bowl and brought the rich-smelling broth to Jonica.

She realized now she felt starved. No meal had ever tasted better than that bowl of broth and she drained it to the last drop.

"Good for you." Her wilderness hostess took the bowl. "Now, I know you want to know everything."

"Please." Jonica swung her legs over the edge of the bunk, sat up and felt her head spin.

"Don't get up," the older woman ordered. Her voice sounded far stronger than when she first invited the visitor in.

"I can't take your bed any longer. I'll be all right after a moment." She forced a smile and waited, head down a bit so blood would rush to her brain and clear it. She glanced at her neatly bound right ankle, surprised at how little it pained but aware the swelling remained.

"Then let me help you to a chair." Sarah trotted over and gave Jonica a little help in getting out of the low bunk. She seated herself in another rocker and smiled. The nurse noticed with pleasure her sharp dark eyes that contrasted strangely with the dull look present when Jonica arrived.

"Now, do you want to tell me who you are and how you happened to find me?" Sarah asked. A look of reverence filled her face. "Although I believe God sent you."

"I do, too. I'm Jonica Carr, an RN, who foolishly got upset and ran away from Seattle instead of sticking it

out and finding the truth. I thought I could get across Stevens Pass and into Leavenworth before the snow got too bad."

Sarah clucked her tongue. "Sounds like we're a real pair."

"Oh?"

"I ran away, too," Sarah confessed, then look shame-faced and chuckled. It brought an answering smile to her guest's lips and she couldn't help exclaiming, "Really?"

"Cross my heart." She solemnly made the childish gesture pledging honesty.

"But why are you here in this awful storm?"

Sarah looked toward the window, shrouded with even more snow. "To prove I'm not a useless old woman." The pain in her voice made Jonica's heart ache.

"I'm sixty-nine years old and ever since I turned sixty-five my family has treated me like a Medicare Casualty. They won't let me do this. They refuse to consider my doing that. 'Be your age, Mother' is their cry—which means sitting in a rocker of their choice, staring at TV and waiting for them to visit when they have time." Twin spots of red marched to her cheeks. "Well, the good Lord's given me a strong, healthy body and my mind is still sound. I rebelled. I got tired of being tucked off in the basement apartment at my daughter's and watching life go on without me. The biggest mistake I ever made was retiring from teaching—although I'd planned to travel."

She signed. "They convinced me to turn over my savings to remodel the basement, another bad decision on my part."

"Like King Lear?"

"No-o." Sarah looked heavenward as if praying for patience. "My children aren't wicked and they would never turn me out. They're just smothering me. Maybe I'm a rebellious old woman but I'm so tired of being set on the shelf just because I've lived a long time."

"You're a perfect dear." Jonica leaned forward and put an impulsive hand over the ones lightly clasped in Sarah's lap. A little idea began in the back of her mind but before she could formulate it, Sarah suddenly laughed ruefully.

"Caught in a net of my own making," she said. "I waited until they went away for a few days, climbed into a car they seldom use and came up here."

"You can *drive* in to this cabin?" The news astonished Jonica.

"A dirt road from Leavenworth," Sarah told her. "I'd planned to sneak back and be in my usual spot when they returned." A frown creased her face. "Now I don't think I can. The first night I got here, I ended up deathly sick, feverish, aching bones, vile headache and retching. It about did me in. Of course, there's no phone here. I could keep a fire going because my son wanted the cabin well-constructed; he uses it during hunting season. I got so weak it scared me but by the next day I felt I could drive if I took it slow. Imagine my dismay when I couldn't get the car started! I suppose since it sits around so much the battery grew weak and standing out in a freezing night didn't help things."

"When was this?" A little twinge went through Jonica. No phone. No car. Continuing storms. At least they had a warm place, food and each other. *Plus God,*

she thought.

Sarah seemed to sense her guest's thought. "I came two days before you arrived. Even when I couldn't get the car going, I didn't worry. Someone would see the smoke from my fire and investigate, although the note I left for my daughter in case they unexpectedly came home sooner than planned just said I'd gone off for a few days." She sighed. "Now everything will be even worse. They'll consider I'm nothing but an irresponsible old woman who needs a keeper." Her face sagged, but the next minute she smiled. "Anyway, the storm swept down and I knew smoke wouldn't rise above the fog and snow, so I just told God, 'You've gotten me out of pickles before. Here I am again.' I knew no one in his right mind would be out here in such weather but I had to do *something*, so I put the kerosene lamp in the window. That way I could pretend someone might come. Besides, if God planned to send help, wouldn't they need a light?"

The long strain, physical exertion and mental turmoil Jonica had gone through exploded into laughter. Sarah's down-to-earth practical approach to God sent the runaway nurse into spasms that shook her body and left her with tear-wet eyes. The near-tragedy for them both had formed a bond more quickly than any other circumstance could do. Jonica finally settled down, wiped her eyes and said, "Sarah Milligan, I know a place that would welcome you. You'd have your own apartment, the choice of cooking your own meals or eating in a dining room, freedom to come and go and the chance for all the giving you want to people who need you."

"Hmmm, sounds like heaven and I'm not ready to go

there." The sharp black eyes reflected unbelief.

"I mean it." Jonica felt her pulse race. "Listen, I have a story you'll love." She began to relate Nicholas Fairchild's experience and how the Shepherd of Love Hospital came to be built. Enthusiasm brought renewed energy and she realized more than ever how much she loved the institution dedicated to those who came. Sarah had heard part of the story but sat entranced at the full tale. Yet when Jonica finished, she shook her head.

"That's all very well, but where's the place for a rebellious old lady?"

"I saved the best for the last. The man who donated the land did so with the stipulation a Retirement Center be built off to one side. It's the place I described. I've toured it and the suites are as attractive and homey as the ones in the staff quarters. In fact, the donor lives there. Permanently."

Sarah looked at her hands, head bowed. "I wouldn't be able to afford it," she confessed in a muffled voice. "All I have is my Social Security and a small teachers' retirement pension. Retirement centers cost money— pots of it. I know. My son and daughter looked at them."

Jonica saw the forlorn, beaten look of a woman who only wanted to be needed. How much she represented thousands of others, victims not of abuse but of over- concern and busy children who had their own lives and families to consider. "Sarah, Nicholas Fairchild built Shepherd of Love for all. Those who can, pay. Those who cannot are still welcome," she gently said.

Some of the fire that had accompanied her recitation about running away jerked the older woman's head erect.

Again, red spots glowed in her cheeks. "How can they do it?"

"Requests for finances are made to God. He opens doors no one knows exist. Unsolicited contributions pour in. Why, right now, Mr. Fairchild and some of the doctors are working to establish a Shepherd of Love Sanctuary and Clinic in the heart of Seattle. It will be built and maintained the same way."

"He must be a wonderful man."

"He is, but so humble that the first time I saw him, I had no idea who he was."

"You said I'd be needed? How?"

"My best nurse friend, Nancy Galbraith, works in Pediatrics. Another, Shina Ito, is in Obstetrics. They tell how frightened children and babies sometimes are. Although the nurses cuddle when they can, their busy schedules simple don't permit time to read stories to and talk with the children and simply rock babies. I know the entire Children's Department would go wild if you appeared. Only thing is, they might just work you to death!"

"Better than rusting from disuse," Sarah retorted but her eyes shone with anticipation. "I suppose there's a waiting list a mile long for the Retirement Center."

"Probably, but if that's where God wants you, it won't matter, will it?"

"No, Jonica, it won't." Sarah sat up straight. "Now you need to get back in bed."

"Not I." She flexed her muscles. "People die in bed. If the storm keeps up, I'll need to have my stamina built up again."

That night after she carefully mounted the little

ladder and settled in the top bunk over Sarah's protests, Jonica listened to the rising wind and snuggled into her warm blankets. By what strange paths God led people into each other's lives. What an asset Sarah would be to the hospital and how everyone would love her! Content in spite of the danger that still lurked, the night charge nurse fell asleep, lulled by the knowledge that Sarah—and God—were nearby.

eleven

"If it weren't that folks must be worrying about us, I'd downright enjoy our visit," Sarah confessed two days later in the midst of another squall.

"I would, too. It's the first time I've had a chance to cook much." Jonica blinked back tears from the onions she had just chopped for a stew. "It's kind of an interlude, a chunk of time between two parts of our lives."

"Well, we have plenty of canned food when we run out of the fresh fruits and vegetables I pilfered from my daughter's refrigerator." She rummaged in a cupboard. "Here's a cake mix and canned frosting. Better than nothing, I s'pose, but you should taste some of my scratch cakes."

"I will when you come to Seattle."

"Am I coming to Seattle?" A hint of laughter in the question.

"You are. Just as soon as there's an opening for you." Jonica clamped down on what she started to add. Until she approached Dr. Peter Hamilton and Emily, she had no right to get Sarah's hopes up. They might prefer keeping their home to themselves while Sarah waited to get into the Retirement Center. On the other hand, Paul would soon be moving into the apartment. Her face warmed, then cooled. Could he ever understand why she had fled and caused all the heartache he must

be experiencing?

"I'll make it up to him," she muttered while Sarah clattered pans and vented her regret in peeling carrots and potatoes.

"What smells better than chocolate cake?" she wondered aloud an hour later. "Isn't it cool enough to cut?"

"Of course." Sarah grinned and eyed the delicious dessert. "Now, I think the stew smells better. So does gingerbread. And pumpkin pie. And fresh hot rolls."

"If I live close to you, I'll look like a roll," Jonica said through a mouth filled with warm cake. "Mmmm. May I have another piece, please?"

Yet cooking didn't take all their time. Neither did tidying up the small space or stoking the fire. The storms continued day after day and with them, the conversational level between the two women deepened. Jonica told Sarah everything starting with her miserable childhood straight through the moment she reached the cabin, guided by that light in the window that stabbed through darkness and beckoned her on when she wondered if she could continue. "If it hadn't shone for me, I would have died," she ended.

"That's how it is with the love of Christ. Millions die spiritually because they don't have His light. Jonica— there's something you need to hear. I probably wouldn't speak if we weren't stranded here waiting for help." She hesitated then went on in her forthright way, dark eyes soft and compassionate. "I've seen your faith increase in the time we've been together but something is holding you back. Is it because you have never forgiven your stepfather—or your mother?"

Jonica flinched. The same thought had haunted her

ever since God led her to safety in the middle of the storm. "I don't think I can do that."

"You must. Just as I must forgive my children, although not for the same reason."

"He doesn't deserve to be forgiven." Memory steeled her voice. "You can't imagine what it was like."

Sarah sat quietly for a long time before saying, "Have you never done anything you felt didn't deserve forgiveness?"

"No, I—" She broke off. "Sarah, that's not a fair question. You know I don't feel Paul should forgive me for doubting him but I want him to. But that's different!"

"Is it, really?" Sarah looked sad, old. "Resentment gnaws away at the person who holds it until she becomes hard and bitter. That's why I ran away. So did you. I know I'm preaching, but think of Jesus hanging on a cross and asking God to forgive those who put Him there. He told us to forgive. Now, my dear, let's talk of happier things. It's been a long time since I visited Seattle. What places will I want to see?"

"Pike Place Market, Mt. Rainier, the Ferry Terminal, the Arboretum, downtown." Jonica enumerated various points of interest.

When she went through the list, Sarah asked, "Tell me more about Shepherd of Love and your friends."

"I could talk about them for hours," she laughingly admitted. "Each of my special nurse friends is different and the difference makes them special. Shina is a combination of Japanese reserve and American fun. Lindsey Best, and she's one of the best surgical nurses I've seen, lives up to her red hair and freckles and big grin. Patty

Thompson is an innocent-looking blond who could talk the birds out of the trees around the hospital but she's also an efficient woman and her young patients adore her. Nancy is—Nancy." Jonica stared into space.

"I have the feeling Nancy carries some childhood or teenage memory as painful as mine. I felt it the first time I met her and a few times have been on the brink of discovering what it is but an interruption or simply Nancy's own reticence has closed the door."

"She's single?"

"Yes. Once I saw her gazing at a Dr. Damon Barton who is in private practice, a children's specialist we call in, attractive. I have a feeling that someday Nancy will share with me, although it's hard. I know." She sighed.

"What about Mrs. Jones-Duncan?" Jonica had long since told Sarah about the trouble the petite woman caused. "Have you forgiven her?"

"It's strange, but I think I have. In the storm she lost importance in my mind. Since then I keep remembering how she looked when she said, 'I can't see that going after the man you love and always have is evil.' I still hate the way she did it, for with the cushion of time and distance since she showed me that note I've come to realize something. If Paul Hamilton really wanted her, he would tell me point-blank. He wouldn't stick with me a minute and excuse himself to Lacy with a made-up alibi that the church wouldn't go for it."

"You are positive now that he loves you, aren't you?"

"I have never been surer of anything in my life except that God loves me even more. Sarah, why did it take me so long to accept it? God's love, then Paul's?" Her poignant cry sounded loud in the little cabin.

"Childhood chains can be strong. It takes time and courage to unlock and free ourselves from them."

Jonica rose and walked to the window she had stared from so many times. "I am really trying to forgive— my stepfather—and—and mother." Hot tears fell. "I want to be free."

"Desire is the first step." Sarah joined her and together they looked out into still another gray, obscuring day. "The seed is planted. Now God will nurture it."

"I've thought a lot and when I get back to Seattle I'm going back. It's been almost eleven years. I've never heard anything or seen either of them. I'm afraid of what I'll find but it has to be done."

"Take your Dr. Paul with you," Sarah advised.

"To that hovel? Never!" Jonica's mouth set in a stubborn line.

"You think he hasn't seen worse? And won't see worse at his Shepherd of Love Sanctuary?" The words hit like ice pellets. "Jonica, your doctor is in the business of providing life and hope to those *exactly like your stepfather*. Who could need it more?"

"That's one reason I've felt so unworthy. I—I don't know if I can work with those kind of people."

"They're created by God, even though they've chosen to follow the devil," Sarah reminded her, but a gentle pat on the shoulder softened the truth. "Besides, when a burden's shared, that burden is halved. I'll be surprised if Dr. Paul isn't overjoyed at the opportunity to take you back so you can begin your healing process, no matter what you find."

"Perhaps." But Jonica stayed at the window staring

blindly past the storm and into her stormy future long after her newfound friend went back to her rocker. When she finally turned, she asked, "Sarah, you were still sick when I came. How could you take care of me?"

One of the sweetest smiles she'd ever seen rested on the other's face. "A body does what she has to. I just told the Lord that since I must be His hands, why, He'd have to increase my strength to be equal to the task. There's a lovely Old Testament blessing in Deuteronomy 33. Moses tells Asher, '. . .your strength will equal your days.' "*

Jonica felt her eyes sting. Would she ever gain the wisdom and peace this spirited woman possessed in abundance? Deep within, she realized these could only come with living. Perhaps going back and facing the past squarely was a beginning.

ॐ

Paul Hamilton stared at the charred remains of what had been Jonica's car, breathing heavily from the climb down to where it lay and weak with relief that his fiancée hadn't been inside. It must have caught fire on impact. A blackened snag, all that remained of a large tree, had crumpled the front end and burned limbs lay on top.

"If it hadn't been for the storm and the road being closed because of the slide, someone would have seen it," said the Search and Rescue leader who grudgingly consented to let Paul come. "Rotten luck."

"It could be a lot worse."

"Yeah." He curiously looked at Paul's drawn face, started to speak and refrained. "Okay, crew, we have work to do."

Paul walked away from the burned car and didn't look

*verse 25 (NIV)

back. In the following hours he learned respect for the thorough team. They scoured every inch of snow-clad ground for clues, although the days and weather since that fateful night offered little to go on. Not until late afternoon did the leader stop.

"We'll take one more ridge, then knock off until morning." He grunted. "Wish this low ceiling would lift. We can't see far enough to catch anything moving."

"After all these days, it isn't likely she'll be moving, is it?" Paul faced the truth and a daggerlike thrust went through him.

"If she found shelter. . . Aw, Doc, you never can tell. Sometimes folks hole up and we find them." Yet the false cheerfulness didn't fool Paul. He wearily trudged after the crew to the top of the little ridge that overlooked a small valley, passionately praying the murk would raise.

It didn't. The Search and Rescue members silently stood and surveyed the limited landscape a long moment, then their leader said, "We'll try again tomorrow."

"Wait!" Paul's voice cracked and he speechlessly pointed. "I thought I saw a light." He forged ahead. Had wishful thinking created the tiny brightness? He sniffed. "Is that smoke?" he called over his shoulder, heart pounding. Light and smoke meant humans. Hampered by the snow, he broke trail, glad for the rough terrain he and his father had hiked over the years in their quest for good fishing spots. He could hear the others floundering behind him, their way made easier by his going. Ten minutes later he stepped onto the porch of an almost-buried cabin, whose single window

held the yellow light he'd seen from afar. "Hello!" He pounded on the door, didn't wait for an answer and lunged through it, snowy and dripping.

His heart sank. A gray-haired woman stared at him from a rocker by the stove. "Who are you?" he cried, hope dying. Oh, God, why hadn't Jonica found this haven?

"Paul."

He whirled toward the whisperer. Tall and pale, Jonica's eyes shone like blue stars. He started toward her, held out his arms, heedless of the snow melting onto the floor, too filled with gratitude to speak or pray. She ran straight into them, lifted her face. He saw regret, tears and more love than he had dreamed possible. With a broken cry she clung to him. His cold lips touched her brown hair, then her lips. When he released her, a rosy blush had driven away her pallor.

"Welcome, Dr. Hamilton." Black eyes twinkled in the older woman's face. "About time you were coming for this girl of yours." She turned to the gaping Search and Rescue crew. "Come in, come in and shut the door. You'll want coffee; Jonica made soup."

"I don't understand." Paul's gaze followed her as she trotted about. "What are you doing here? How long have *you* been here, Jonica? How did you find this cabin out in the middle of nowhere?" He hugged her to make sure he wasn't dreaming.

"Sarah's lamp in the window shone through the darkness. I followed it. She took care of me." What a few words to express all that had happened. Paul knew the whole story would come later. For now, it was enough to have found his lost fiancée. For the first time he

realized a little of what Jesus must have felt when he found unharmed the sheep who had wandered from His fold. And what He felt every time a strayed sheep returned.

"Shuck off those wet coats," Sarah ordered. "Goodness, what a mess." She reached for a mop but the team leader beat her to it.

"Go back on the porch and shake off the snow," he ordered. "You, too, Doc. It won't do any good to find your nurse, then have her catch pneumonia from getting soaked."

Paul's laugh rang out. He obediently followed the others out, rid his jacket of most of the snow then came back in, laughing to see how efficiently the leader attacked the puddles on the floor.

A half hour later, reasonably warm and dry, the Search and Rescue crew left. "We'll bring a new battery," they promised. "Sure you don't want to go with us, Doc?"

He coolly looked into their grinning countenances. "If you were in my shoes, would you?"

"Naw." They shrugged into their coats and went out, still laughing.

"Now." Paul looked first at Sarah Milligan, then at Jonica. "I want to hear the whole story."

It took a long time, with the women sometimes filling in for one another. Paul's relief knew no bounds. "Sarah, thank God you are just what you said—a rebellious woman." He eliminated the word *old*. No one with her spirit would ever be anything but ageless.

Jonica quickly told him of their plans for her rescuer's move to Seattle and he saw the eagerness in Sarah's lined face. He determined to do everything possible to

get her into the Retirement Center as soon as possible. "In the meantime," he suggested, to Jonica's amazement and delight. "Why don't you come stay with Dad and Emily? I know they'll love having you and you can get started loving those children who need you so much."

She seemed to grow taller. "Dr. Paul, you will never know until you're my age how much those words mean. Oh, to be needed again! It's just this side of heaven." Unashamed tears crept from her eyes.

"Will your son and daughter object?"

"Probably, but I'm still their mother, although the last few years they've tried to turn things around." Her lips set for battle and her black eyes flashed. "I know it's because they love me but now I'll be free."

"Free," Jonica repeated wistfully when Sarah had considerately gone to the bottom bunk and turned with her face away from the two who sat with rockers close enough for them to whisper confidences without someone else listening. "Paul, if you knew how much I regret running away."

He took her hands in his and looked deep into her eyes. Flickering shadows from the turned-down lamp in the window couldn't hide their expression. "My darling, about the note—"

"I know it couldn't mean what she said." Perfect trust illumined her features.

The last unspoken question as to why she hadn't believed in him fled forever. To think she loved him that much, had the faith he would never betray her, after a life in which she had been subject to betrayal by those who should have cherished her. Humbled, he

tightened his grip, hating to bring Lacy's name into the secure little cabin but knowing he must. "She wanted to have the church sponsor a benefit dance. My note told her how impossible the scheme was and to forget it."

"And I accepted that you—" The low, repentant cry tore from Jonica's throat. "Can you ever forgive me?"

"It's over. All of it." In whispers he told her of the blond woman's frantic call, her reception when he went to her empty mansion, his feeling that perhaps she had learned a lesson. He ended by saying, "Jonica, are you ready to leave the past? Will you marry me as soon as we can get home and arrange it?" The word *again* hung unspoken in the air. To his surprise, Jonica slowly shook her head. "Sarah—and God—have made me see I can't go into the future until the past is truly settled." She took a long, quivering breath but her gaze never left his. "Paul, I've accepted God the way I should have done a long time ago when I went through the form but had little concept of His love. Before I marry you, I need to go see my mother and stepfather." She paused. "Will you go with me?"

The forlorn look that so reminded him of a hurt child cut him to the heart. He stood, pulled her up so he could put his arms around her and whispered into her ear, "Nothing on earth can keep me from it. We'll go the minute we get home and cleaned up." He felt her tense body relax and heard the little sob, then turned her toward the bunk beds. "Get some sleep, dear. Tomorrow's going to be a long day."

She climbed the little ladder and settled into the top bunk. Paul lay down on his bed on the floor, marveling

that Sarah could have slept there. Or had she slept? Probably not. He'd just bet she spend most of the night caring for Jonica. Why hadn't the woman he loved been born to a mother like Sarah? Yet, who was he to question God's ways? Good would come out of evil every time. God had promised it. Paul fell asleep with a prayer on his lips, not only of thankfulness but that Jonica would receive strength for whatever appalling condition they might encounter when she retraced the painful steps to her childhood.

twelve

The following morning help arrived, along with clear winter skies and a rise in temperature that set the eaves of the little cabin dripping. Search and Rescue personnel brought a new battery, installed it in Sarah's car and over-ruled her insisting she could perfectly well drive back to Leavenworth. "Right on our way, ma'am," they told her and grinned. By early afternoon she'd been delivered to a sputtering but relieved daughter and family after a whispered promise to come to Seattle if the older Hamiltons were willing.

Jonica hugged her and watched the car drive out of sight, feeling bereft, hating to see her staunch friend go.

"It won't be long." Paul promised. Yet she stayed quiet until they reached the spot where he had parked his car and joined the Search and Rescue crew. She noticed he pressed bills into the reluctant hands and she thanked each one individually.

"If the Doc here doesn't treat you right, you let us know," the leader told her. He chuckled. "Although there's no chance of that. If you could have seen his face when he looked at the burned car. . ." He shook his head, eyes sober. "That God you believe in sure took good care of you."

"He takes care of all who believe in Him," she told him. "If you don't believe me, try Him and find out

for yourself."

"I will." He turned away. "Thanks."

She watched him go through a mist. How caring and giving Search and Rescue men and women were! They braved dangers on behalf of others and their jobs called for steady nerves. She offered a prayer on their behalf. If they added faith to their efforts—and perhaps many of them did—results might be even better.

With all her heart she wanted to stay awake on the drive home. She couldn't. Head pillowed against Paul's strong right arm and feeling that nothing could ever again harm her, she fell asleep just west of the summit and didn't awaken until they pulled into the hospital lot. "Why, where's the snow?" Eyes accustomed to everlasting white, the sun-washed February hospital grounds looked bare and unfamiliar.

"In the mountains where it belongs." Paul chuckled, unfastened his seat belt and stepped out. A few moments later he unlocked her outside door, led her in and said, "Take a warm bath and sleep. I'll let Nancy and the others know we're back, although Search and Rescue promised to notify Dad last night, so they probably already know. I also called on the car phone while you slept."

"I've slept enough." Jonica wouldn't put the inevitable off any longer. "Paul, if I bathe, can we eat and find mother? I have a terrible feeling of urgency, as if she needs me."

Paul didn't discount it. They had both known of too many cases where an inner warning signal meant something important. "Can you be ready in an hour?"

"Yes." She caught a glimpse of herself in a mirror.

Tousled, but rested-looking, eyes wide. Her parka smelled of smoke and needed a good cleaning. Her stained slacks would make good rags. "Goodness, what an awful looking person!"

He cocked one eyebrow in the way she found endearing, snatched a kiss and went out the hall door. She heard him knock on Nancy's door and a moment later her beautiful friend entered.

"I'll run your bath. Get out of your soiled clothing and leave it in a pile."

How like Nancy not to insist on hearing the story when Jonica needed her ministering hands! Again came a feeling that one day she would learn what lay beneath the surface of Nancy Galbraith. She gratefully accepted the skilled nurse's help in shampooing her hair. "No wonder the children love you," she said. "You're so gentle."

Nancy rinsed her hair, toweled it and waited until Jonica slipped into a robe before leading her to a low chair and blow-drying the brown hair. "Paul said you are going to find your mother. What do you want to wear?"

Jonica considered, remembering the slovenly area she'd grown up in. "Something cheerful but not too bright."

Nancy flipped through her wardrobe and held up a soft yellow sweater and dark blue slacks. She added a lined navy windbreaker, warm enough for the evening, and navy walking shoes. "How about these?"

"Fine." Jonica ran her tongue over lips dry from dread. "I—I don't know if I can do this but I have to," she confessed when she finished dressing.

"Would you like to pray about it?"

"I don't think any words will come out."

Nancy put her arm around the troubled nurse. "Then I'll pray." She hesitated and Jonica felt some of her friend's calm spirit enter her own heart.

"Our dear heavenly Father, we thank You for being with us wherever we go. We are grateful You brought Jonica safely home. Now we ask that You will go with her—no, go before her, in this hard task and that your Holy Spirit will guard and guide her. In Jesus' precious name, amen."

"Amen," Jonica whispered.

The fragile moment of sharing ended when a rap at the door announced Paul's arrival. She ran to it, saw the way his dark eyes lighted when he saw her. Clean shaven and scrubbed, he'd chosen gray slacks and jacket with a pale blue shirt. "Ready?"

She looked from him to Nancy's encouraging brown eyes. Strength flowed into her body. She took Paul's hand. "I'm ready."

The street she used to know had grown even seedier. Broken windows in vacant houses showed some residents had fled. A group of youths on a nearby corner stared in their direction, muttered something to one another and laughed. Jonica felt her face scorch. Only too well did she know the kind of street humor such individuals chose to impress one another. Yet, as Sarah said, they were part of God's creation in spite of their sins. She felt sweat start and her hands grew clammy. Facing the past was even worse than she had expected. She longed to cry out, to plead with Paul to take her away. Yet if she did, it meant separation in their

marriage forever. This area wasn't far from the Shepherd of Love Sanctuary already on its foundation and rising as rapidly as skilled crews could work.

"Turn here." She motioned to a short street that angled off right. The same desolation prevailed.

"Which house?" Sympathy colored Paul's voice and she caught the admiration mingled with uncertainty. This couldn't be easy for him either.

"Last on the left."

He parked across the broken street and Jonica stared at the house. It looked smaller than she remembered, with an overgrown yard and sagging steps. She clutched Paul's hand when they walked to the door. Her mouth twisted. For one of the few times ever, no sound of cursing and quarreling greeted her. Perhaps they had moved away. No, Paul's knock brought the sound of shuffling feet. The door opened a crack. A voice Jonica had never forgotten demanded, "Who are you and what do you want?"

"Mother?" She strained to see the woman through the torn screen.

Silence greeted her, the silence of shock. The door opened wider. An emaciated replica of the woman Jonica remembered stood before her, shoulders bent, eyes surprisingly alive. "Jonica?"

"Yes, Mother." Like one in a daze she stepped inside and fearfully glanced around. Why, where were the alcohol and tobacco fumes that had permeated the house until her clothes reeked? Where was the blaring TV? Only a sagging daybed, a shabby refrigerator and stove and one chair graced the cheerless room. Jonica gaped at their cleanliness.

"He's gone. He died of alcoholism years ago."

She turned back to her mother, a wave of relief threatening to overwhelm her.

"I tried to find you, after—" The too-old face worked. "No one knew where you were." Anguished tears made a steady stream. "Can you ever forgive me?" She held out trembling hands to the daughter she had tried to protect even in her own misery and weakness. "I never blamed you for going. I couldn't control him much longer." She tottered to the daybed and fell on to it. One hand went to her heart.

Paul sprang to her side. "I'm a doctor and your daughter is a nurse. We'll help you."

Jonica saw the involuntary brightening of her mother's wan face when Paul said *daughter*. Why hadn't she come back sooner? Why hadn't she faced her dragon, which now turned out to be in her own mind?

"Stay with her. I'll call an ambulance from the car phone." Paul sprinted out.

Jonica loosened her mother's clothing, found an old but clean towel and wet it from the kitchen faucet. By the time the ambulance from Shepherd of Love arrived, her mother had rallied but blue shadows beneath her eyes told their own story of poverty, malnutrition and abuse of the fluttering heart. She clutched Jonica's hand all during the ride and tried to speak but her daughter's firm hand and negative headshake caused her to subside.

"Will you do what's necessary?" Jonica asked Paul when they reached the hospital.

"I will." Yet when he finished an examination he came to her with a worried look. "She needs heart surgery.

Shall we transfer her or shall I perform it? Or shall we call in another surgeon?" He placed both hands on her shoulders. "Jonica, she a very sick woman. Would you be more comfortable knowing someone else performed the operation if she dies? Right now, she's in God's hands and needs everything we can do."

Jonica stared blindly at him, feeling his strong, capable fingers press into her shoulders. Yet she didn't hesitate. "If I can put my life in your hands, I can put my mother's there, too. Besides, as you say, it's really God's hands, isn't it?"

"Good girl." He kissed her and hurried to the operating theatre where Emily Davis Hamilton, Lindsey Best and a full complement of medical personnel had assembled to prepare for the task ahead.

Part of Jonica wanted to remain with her mother. The more sensible side told her it wouldn't be wise. Already unnerved from the gamut of physical and emotional stress she had been subjected to in the last weeks, even her trained mind could play false. She must not take the chance of making the slightest sound that could distract the single-hearted team. So during the long hours, Jonica learned what waiting meant. How often her heart had gone out to those who helplessly sat by while a loved one hovered between life and death. Now she experienced it firsthand. A blessed numbness protected her from some of the pain but it also prevented her from praying. Yet she took comfort knowing God could read her heart.

Paul found her huddled in a corner of the surgical suite staring blindly at the wall. "She came through, darling."

The dam broke. Tears stored up since childhood cas-

caded. Paul held her close and let her cry. Tears brought healing.

"Is she really going to be all right?" Jonica finally asked.

"There is still risk. She's rundown and in poor physical health. We still have a fight on our hands but there's a good chance we can win." He stopped and held her away until he could look into her eyes. "I believe if she had gone through this surgery before she saw you, she wouldn't have survived."

Jonica sagged in his arms. "What do you mean?"

"You know as well as I how determination often makes all the difference." He swallowed hard. "You have given her something to live for. The last thing she said before receiving anesthesia was, 'I have to make it so my daughter will forgive me.' I told her, 'she already has.' I've never seen a more beautiful smile on a human face. Her body relaxed and made our job easier."

Emily continued her duties as night charge nurse so Jonica could be with her mother. She was there when first consciousness returned, using her skills to comfort. She prayed aloud beside her mother's bed and felt the blessing of a frail hand on her hair, as it had been so many years ago. She watched color come into the pale face and laughed when her mother finished everything on her tray and demanded more.

"We've wasted too much time," she said simply. A little frown crossed her forehead and she said half shyly, "Jonica, I can't go back."

"You never will. You'll be transferred to Intermediate Care when you're able and I promise, you'll never go

back." Yet her mother's expression brought a little worry. Jonica discussed it with Paul. "I've just found her again. How can I leave her?" She felt pulled like a wishbone. "Paul, I want to marry you, but what about Mother?"

"We have to pray about it," Paul said soberly. A few days later, he pounded on her door and caught her around the waist when she let him in. "God is so good!"

"Of course He is, but what has He done now?"

"Nothing but to solve everything." Paul sounded like an eager boy. His mussed dark hair and glowing dark eyes made him look more like a high school senior than an eminent surgeon. "I've been haunting the Director of our Retirement Center and just learned something ver-r-ry interesting." He laughed and freed her enough until they could sit down on the couch in her pretty blue and white room. "There is an opening and for one reason or another, everyone on the waiting list has turned it down; a few have moved and others decided to live with their families. This means Sarah has her suite ready and waiting."

"That's wonderful!" Jonica felt genuine gladness. "But—"

"It also means she won't be living with Dad and Emily. They're disappointed, after all the good things they heard about her. I think they've been planning ways to keep her and her good cooking, especially since Emily will be embroiled in the Sanctuary. Anyway, they'd like to have your mother come to them after she is well enough to care for herself; to rest and decide where she wants to be—hopefully, in the Retirement Center when another suite's available. She and Sarah will hit it off like ham and eggs."

"It's such a pat ending it sounds like a novel where the author works everything around so everyone has a 'happily ever after,'" Jonica said.

"My dear woman, if authors can do that in books, why should it surprise us that the Author of life itself keeps His promises? 'And we know that all things work together for good to them that love God, to them who are the called according to his purpose,'* Paul tells the Romans. Notice how he doesn't just say *called*. He says *the called*. I've always felt that meant those who recognize and accept His calling." Paul's face glowed. "Don't you see? Everything that has happened, each step of our lives, has been part of His plan and built a foundation for the next step."

Jonica caught his train of thought. Her blue eyes opened wide. Her heart beat fast with new understanding. "If I hadn't come here and met you, if I hadn't run away and found Sarah—" She felt on the verge of great knowledge. "Why, Paul, I never would have gone back. Mother would have died alone without God and part of me would have stayed hard and dead. I could never have supported you or worked with you at the Sanctuary."

"Can you now, my darling?" The last barrier stood between them, waiting to be reinforced by her scars or torn down by unquestioning faith in God.

A hundred thoughts raced through Jonica's mind and heart. The way her mother had begun to listen to the scriptures. Sullen faces of idle youth grouped on broken sidewalks. Sad-faced children, all with faces like her own, cringing from many kinds of abuse. Dirt. Poverty. Hopelessness. Alcoholism. Drugs. The lamp

*Romans 8:28 (KJV)

Sarah had placed in her window that shone into the darkness and helped save Jonica's life.

> *Neither do men light a candle, and put it under a bushel, but on a candlestick; and it giveth light unto all that are in the house.*
>
> *Let your light so shine before men, that they may see your good works, and glorify your Father, which is in heaven. ** *

Verses learned years ago because it was expected of her. Now Jonica realized the depth of their call, the responsibility they placed on every soul who enlisted in the Lord's service.

Many lit candles in sterile hospitals, clean surroundings, among hurting men, women and children. The scripture implied that when the candle had been lit and put in the candlestick, it must be carried to the darkest corners so that the entire house could glow with the light of the gospel. Kerosene lamps, candles, flashlights, torches, operating room lights. All gave their rays according to the power they possessed when lit or turned on. Jesus, the Light of the world, must be taken where most needed.

Jonica passed one hand over her eyes. She felt she had finished a long journey and could never again be the same person. Blackness of soul had been erased. She looked out her window. A single ray of sunlight bathed the grounds in rose before evening shadows fell. She turned to Paul. "With God at our side, I can."

❧

Two weeks later a small group gathered in the hospital

*Matthew 5:15,16 (KJV)

Chapel. Hothouse roses delicately perfumed the air. Nicholas Fairchild and the Hospital Director, the Hamiltons, Lindsey, Patty, Shina, Nancy with her quiet smile, Sarah and a few others, including Paul's friend Garry Sterling, filled the small area. Dr. Paul stood in front, tall and handsome next to the minister. A little rustle at the back turned heads. Jonica, lovely and gowned in the simplest of wedding dresses, gently helped her mother up the aisle, seated her next to Peter Hamilton, bent over and kissed her. She straightened, wanting to memorize every detail of the ceremony in which God would join her life with Paul's forever. A tall white candle stood next to a polished, but old, kerosene lamp, surrounded by greenery and roses.

She smiled, saw the ardor in Paul's dark eyes, the love that beckoned and warmed her. Then she walked toward him and the circle of light in which he stood waiting.

You can meet Nancy, Jonica, Dr. Paul and the others again in Shepherd of Love Hospital Series: Book Two, *Flickering Flames*, coming soon from HEARTSONG PRESENTS.